JUST PRETEND

An Accidental Text Fake Engagement Romance

Love Comes to Town Book 3

ASHLEE PRICE

https://www.ashleepriceromanceauthor.com/

CHAPTER 1

Nolan

"You have to be married in three months," Emerson blurts out.

I stare at him.

Married... three months...

The words don't seem to go together.

Emerson is still tracing that infinity symbol into the chocolate cake remnants on his plate, but there's almost no chocolate left. His stainless-steel fork is scraping across one of the porcelain plates we got a deal on from some supplier that was going out of business and remembered a favor Dad did for them once upon a time. But the main thing is that what he just said, that crazy talk, was out-of-fucking-bounds and im-fucking-possible.

Dad wouldn't have put in such a useless, out-of-left-field requirement. He just wouldn't.

His voice echoes in my head: "Don't end up like me, Nolan boy, old, sad, alone and regretful. You find yourself a good girl, you stick with her, no matter what. Even when it's hard."

I scowl, even though it's my own dumb-ass brain bringing back these blasts from the past.

C'mon, that was one late night in some weird underground speakeasy when Dad was drunk on this terrible wine from Greenland, of all places, and had just found out that Mom had remarried.

"Nolan?" Landon prompts.

I can feel his gaze nudging me to look at him. But I can hear the sympathy in his voice, and I don't want to see it in his face. I don't want his fucking sympathy.

Kyra and Harley just look sad, like I'm a puppy dog who got kicked, who they might give a hug if I so much as sniffle. Although a hug is the last thing I need right now.

Whatever Emerson—the most honest brother of all of us—said, it can't be true.

"You can't be serious," I say lightly.

To think I actually bought it for a second there. I guess I had this coming, though; with all the pranks and jokes I've pulled on my brothers over the years—Landon's still pissed about those shrimp tails I hid in his curtain rod that took him a good two months to find—they were bound to seek retribution sometime.

Although I can't say this is their best work. Out of all the shit they could've claimed Dad specified in his will, there's about a thousand things that I would've bought before this: Dad having about twelve illegitimate children he's leaving money to, Dad having learned he's the son of Putin and wanting us to visit him, a pet polar bear for each of us. But not this. No fucking way.

"You've got to be kidding me," I insist.

But none of them—Greyson, Harley, Emerson, Kyra—will meet my eye. As for Landon... when I finally meet his eye, the expression there is as good as a condemnation.

"No fucking way," I hiss, although this time it's nothing more than sheer denial.

30 minutes earlier...

Sometimes all it takes is a glimpse. For Sierra Hill, it took even less.

Not that I know it yet—I don't have a fucking clue.

Right now, she's just a split-second once-over: hot little Coke-bottle body, brown-red hair the color of that delicious red velvet cake Mom used to make us for our birthdays, blue startled eyes, the curling of a generous lower lip that could be the cousin to a smile.

Yeah, a half-second glimpse that ends with me knowing. Not her name, not yet.

Just that I want what I see.

Too bad now's not a good time. It's a really fucking shitty time, actually.

Tonight's not about me. Although maybe later, once the dinner's over...

Tearing my gaze off her as she continues to the bathroom, I raise my glass and my smile to the others at the table. "Here's to my brother and his love—may you be as happy as you look."

Everyone chuckles, although Landon shoots me a glare.

I just wink. "You almost make being engaged look palatable."

Something's been up with him tonight. Something that's making his responses come seconds too late, his smiles too. Something that he's not saying.

We're at the Miller comedy club and restaurant, although the comedy club is out of commission. It's under renovation—renovations which I'm overseeing, unfortunately. Normally, I like construction and supervising, but this project has been plagued by one mishap after another.

Right now, Landon's bringing the back of Kyra's hand to his lips, affection kindling in his hazel eyes. "What can I say—this girl makes it easy."

She chuckles with a toss of her dark-haired head, before leaning in for a kiss. "You smooth-talker, you."

I glance away, but the woman from before is long gone, of course. Not that it matters much. You catch one, you lose one—was that what Dad used to say after he and Mom called it quits and he embarked on his epic dating spree that culminated in some Victoria's Secret model, and that the rest of us have yet to match?

Not that my other brothers are really trying. Greyson, the eldest, is married and has a kid. Even goddamn Landon, who I had pegged for a forever bachelor like myself after his university love debacle, ended up engaged to said university love debacle—hence the whole reason for this dinner—and with a kid. Emerson is still loyal to the bachelor cause, but who knows for how long, with this new Polish girlfriend—Monica, Molly, Maude—that he won't shut up about.

Landon's started on me too, lately, with the odd suggestion I find my own 'Kyra' here, the Dad-esque comments that I can't be a bachelor forever there. Weird.

Hell, Landon has always been the 'Responsible Twin', but now that he knows he's a father it seems like that's translated into him as the 'Responsibly Annoying Twin'. Jesus. I can't even remember the last time all of us brothers went out on the town together and got shitfaced.

"The place is looking good for being under renovation," Emerson says, with a look around.

I swallow back the urge to point out that this front restaurant area is the only one we'll be keeping open for now, and strictly by necessity. And that once we're finished with it, the yawn-worthy stucco walls and cement parking-garage-esque floor will be replaced by something unrecognizable. Something my overzealous and overpaid designer Melinda assured me would be 'WOW'. She did show me a bunch of pictures of her 'mood board' for the area that didn't make me want to vomit, so we were a go.

"You should see the back," I grumble instead.

"That bad, eh?" he says, all sympathetic connivance.

That's the thing about my little brother, God bless him. He isn't good at pretending he cares—he does one better: he actually cares.

"We're months behind and will probably be months more behind, thanks to fucking Gerard's mishaps," I mutter, eyeing the bar warily.

That asshole spent more time here drinking than he did working, and it came across in his completely fucked measurements for every room. Tool didn't even apologize, either. I finally fired the idiot, but not before his fuck-ups cost us months, at least. Dickwad.

I give my head a little shake. "Anyway, it's good to be here with everyone." I gesture at Landon and Kyra. "And look at those two lovebirds."

"Picked where you'll be heading for the honeymoon?" Emerson asks the happy couple, smiling over the rim of his wineglass at them. I'm pretty sure that's his third glass.

For all his mooning over this M chick, he has started drinking more since he's been seeing her.

"We're just trying to get through the wedding first," Kyra confesses with a happy little laugh.

Landon gives her an even happier kiss. Christ, I know they're in loooove, but how many times can you feel like kissing the same person in a matter of consecutive minutes? "By 'we', she means 'her'. One quick visit with the wedding planner was all it took for us to figure out that I have zero taste."

He says that like hemming and hawing for hours over napkin shapes and doily fabrics is anything other than an elaborate 20th century form of male torture.

"Babe," Kyra says, a smile cracking on her red lips, "you were going to have our color scheme be gray and silver."

"I stand by what I said," Landon states stoutly. "Sensible colors, both of them."

The rest of us chuckle. I try to keep my face lighter than my thoughts: that what Landon's doing is anything but sensible. Yeah, Greyson and Harley make the whole marriage thing look easy, but they've been at it a little over a year. And sure, Landon has been in love with Kyra since forever, but when was that ever a recipe for marital bliss?

What he should be doing is what I'm doing: taking a page out of Mommy and Daddy dearests' marriage handbook and see the whole thing as the losing game it is.

I nudge Greyson and ask him in an undertone, "Chosen a gift yet? I call dibs on that panda onesie for that kid."

"Her name's Madison," he grumbles. "And she's eight. That link you sent me could fit a five-year-old, maybe."

"I know what her name is," I grumble back. "I'm her favorite uncle, remember? And anyway, that's what zippers are for: squeezing into outfits that aren't a perfect fit. Plus, when she gets like, I don't know, sixteen or something, she can donate that beauty of an outfit to Dakota."

"Wonderful," Greyson says, running a hand through his coiffed dark hair.

"Oh stop," Harley says to him, a half-grin showing the gap between her front teeth. Her sandy blonde hair is gathered in two fishtail braids that would look ridiculous on anyone else. "That panda outfit is hilarious." She cranes up her head so that her chin rests on his shoulder with a knowing smile. "Besides, you're just grumpy because…" As his scowl grows, she trails off, moving away with a shake of her head. "Forget it."

"Forget what?" I ask. Tonight is starting to annoy me, and it's not just that someone went all fruity scented candle-happy with our tables in the two hours I left to go home and veg out. "Seems like everyone's in on some bad news I don't know about. Or are you all still pissed that I skipped Dad's will reading? I told you, batty old Aunt Edna has it in for me."

I stifle a shudder. Her and most of Dad's extended family. They being majorly old-fashioned means that one look at my tattooed, long-haired self will send any one of them into a days-long rant about 'kids these day'. Never mind that I'm thirty-fucking-two.

"Oh, speaking of," Emerson chimes in, light blond head bowed as he digs through the leather messenger bag he has slung on his chair. "She wanted me to give you these." He takes out a familiar Barney-purple tin bedecked with gaudy golden lettering and I groan.

"You see? Does she give anyone else eons-expired chocolate mints from the '70s? No, I think not."

The others crack up, although I'm not finished yet. I take the tin and give it a shake, suspiciously eyeing its bottom. Most of the lettering is faded and I can't seem to find a manufacture date, which isn't necessarily a promising sign.

I pause, my suspicious glance moving on to them. Normally, one of them chimes in to defend the old witch—after all, she usually gives them a crisp hundred-dollar bill on every occasion ranging from Halloween to Hanukkah, despite the fact that we aren't Jewish, and she does play a mean game of table tennis.

Hell, something's definitely up.

"OK, no shit," I tell him. "Spill. What's this shitty secret of yours?"

Greyson, Landon and Emerson exchange a look.

"Don't tell me," I grumble. "Dad had some more surprises in his will."

Not that I'm overly worried. Our father-son relationship might have been rocky in my teen years, but it ended up OK. I did go into business at Storm Inc. how he wanted, after all. Sure, it was part-time, and sure, I focused more on my comedy career, but still. Plus, Dad was never stingy with us—just a bit strict, that was all.

Even if in business, he was as slippery as an eel.

All things considered, at the end of the day, he was a good dad, and a shitty human being. If I didn't know any better, I'd think that I missed him.

Who knows, maybe I do. Maybe.

"Now isn't really the time," Greyson is saying carefully, his jaw tensed, gesturing to Landon and Kyra. After all, this dinner is to celebrate them.

"Don't hold back on account of me," Landon says, taking a sip of his water as he eyes the others. "The sooner Nolan knows, the better."

"I don't know...." is all Emerson contributes uncertainly, twiddling his spoon.

I'm about ready to brandish my knife at these doofuses. They know how much I hate being out of the loop, and they pull this?

Instead, I grit my teeth together, place the flat of both palms on the table, and, in a voice so calm motherfucking Buddha would give me props, say, "The sooner Nolan knows what, the better?"

I've had about as much of this as I can take. Yes, it's supposed to be a celebratory dinner for Landon and his perfect relationship with his high school sweetheart, but fuck it, my brothers just need to tell me what's up and get it over with.

"It's Dad's will," Greyson says, his face already sympathetic. "He's leaving everything to us equally—but yours has a condition."

All of a sudden, everyone at the table looks away, as if I have scabby leprosy or some shit.

"Which is?" I say.

I might as well pull this Band-Aid off nice and fast.

But they're all sitting there speechless, as if saying it is as good as starting a countdown to my demise.

Emerson is carving a chocolaty infinity symbol into the remnants of his chocolate mousse cake. Landon's hazel-eyed gaze on me is assessing, as if trying to track my response already. Greyson's sculpted face is blank; he's probably playing footsie under the table with that wife of his. Meanwhile, my brain churns over what it could be. Some kind of stupid ethics course? A forced visit to clean up that island we always suspected he had? He found out about my casino loss all those years ago and is instating a ban?

"Guys," I growl.

"You have to be married in three months," Emerson blurts out.

CHAPTER 2

Sierra

I wonder what he's thinking about now.

That guy from before—that man. The one whose muscled tattooed arms rested on the back of the seat in a casual lounge that seemed at odds with the fire kindling in his hazel eyes. My mind goes back to that moment: how the square of his face was angled towards me, his lips pursed.

Why, hello there.

Not that it mattered. It was just a moment, a glance. I'll probably never see him again.

"Helloooo, earth to Sierra?" Josie waves a hot pink and neon green fingernailed hand in front of my face. "Have you heard one word of what I said?"

"Huh? Yeah, I totally…" I trail off, racking my brain. "OK, I might have missed a bit."

Wynona snorts, then takes a slurp of her chocolate milkshake, her lips leaving a black lipstick smear on the straw when she's done.

"Can you really blame me?" I protest. "You guys have been grumbling about the guys here for at least an hour. If this was supposed to be a Scope Mission, then why didn't we hit up O'Malley's or any of our usual spots?"

"Because," Josie says, fluttering her strawberry-blonde lashes as if it's the most obvious thing in the world, "we go to the usual spots, we'll see the usual boys. And you heard Wynona: we don't want boys. We want men."

Now it's my turn to snort. I pick up a spoon and brush aside the chunk of side-bang that's been annoying me to hell and making me seriously consider just saying fuck it and chopping it off. "Boys are men are boys. Just because a man is an asshat, you call him a boy, and vice versa."

"Um, excuse me," Josie says, using her ice cream spoon as a baton and pointing it at me with her pink gloss lips drawn into a disapproving frown. "We are supposed to be here for moral support for Wynona, not for you to—"

"I knew it," Wynona cuts in, pale pointed chin sinking to the table so that her choppy bowl cut bangs settle over her face like dyed black protective wings. "I knew it would all go to shit."

"There, there," Josie says, shoving her half-finished bowl of strawberry sprinkle ice cream in front of her sister. "Jeremy was just a jerkwad, and you'll meet a better one. Promise."

Her warning glare at me forces a half-hearted "promise" out of me too.

Although Josie knows how I feel about the subject. The three of us have been friends since forever and have been brutally honest with each other since forever too. I don't know when that stopped extending to Wynona's piss-poor taste in men, but somewhere along the way it did. And now we tiptoe around the subject, as if it's a shock that the latest unemployed asshole with a criminal record turns out to be an asshole once again.

I sniff the air with a light smile. Last time I was here was years ago, but I definitely don't remember the smell: is that spiced apple? I guess the little red heart-shaped candles on our table aren't just for show.

Weird, in a comedy club, but I'm not complaining. At least, now I'm not. We originally went here expecting the comedy club part of this place to be open, to help cheer Wynona up, but had to settle for just food instead.

"There's no one here," Wynona moans out of her hair temple.

"Stop that," Josie says sternly. It's almost funny sometimes, how unlike they are for twins. With all of Wynona's piercings, makeup, dark dyed hair, and tattoos, they don't even really look alike anymore. "There's a whole table of perfectly eligible men at the back. I saw them myself."

"All with their wives slash girlfriends," Wynona says stoutly. "I saw."

I pat her back gingerly, while Josie mouths to me, too much wine.

"Unless they are all married to the same two women, that's doubtful," Josie trills peppily. "And one totally looked like your type. Long hair, tattoos."

"Probably a wife-beater," Wynona grumbles glumly.

I'm inclined to agree with her, but hold myself back.

With just about everything else in life, Wynona's killing it. She's the top tattoo artist in New York, has saved up enough to have a chic flat that Josie and I drool over, has abs that make me seriously consider going to the gym, and her Dalmatian's obedience makes me practically die in shame every time Horatio and I come over for a visit.

Right now, though, she's a mess. So, it's really not the time to break it to her.

No, I just need to wait for one of the very often times she has her shit together and is sober, and drop the bomb: Over the past year, after Gary dumped you, your taste in men has gone from bad to worse. Very worse.

Not that I'm some relationship expert myself.

"Maybe we should go to O'Malley's," Josie suggests, reaching for her rapidly melting ice cream and taking a bite thoughtfully. She offers a spoonful to me. "Want some?"

"Sure." I take a bite myself. "I could use the fuel. Skipped breakfast and over lunch I was so busy shooting out emails to prospective clients that I only ate half a muffin."

Blue eyes widening, Josie lowers her spoon as her mouth becomes a guilty O... with the result that pink ice cream slops onto the table.

"Shit." She mops it up with one of the napkins Wynona hasn't yet blown her nose on. "God, sorry, I've been so wrapped up in..." She trails off, waving to Wynona, as if there was any doubt what she meant. "How are things going? The job hunt, I mean."

I shrug. "Shittily. I might actually have to go back to the Pancake House."

Josie drops her napkin. "No. Don't say that."

I sigh. "Why not? It's the truth. I'm beginning to loathe ramen, and I'm not going to my mom."

"But the Pancake House..." Josie's horrified expression says it all.

"Maybe Raymond isn't there anymore?" I try.

She scoffs. "Yeah, he only owned the whole place."

I shrug, reaching for the ice cream and taking a yummy strawberry bite for myself. "Well, he'd take me back, at least."

She yanks it back to herself with a glare, although we both know it's not over the ice cream. "Yeah, so he could grope you and make all those creepy comments about what he'd like to do with those 'pretty feet of yours'."

At her rendition of him—low voice and creepy as hell—we all crack up, even Wynona.

"Guess I should've known what to expect when he had us wear sandals at a pancake house," I say, trying to sound more chagrined than resigned.

When I walked out of its yellow and red striped doors, I swore I'd never set foot in the place again, and now I'm actually…

"Stop," Josie declares. "Not another word. I forbid it."

"You can't forbid it," I point out.

"I forbid it," she repeats, more forcefully this time, stabbing her ice cream spoon at me before getting herself another spoonful. "You, Sierra Hill, are a journalist. And you will accept nothing less."

"Even if it means me living on the street?"

Mouth full of ice cream, Josie grumbles, "For the billionth time, you can come live with me. Or Wyn. Right, Wyn?"

At the sullen silence that greets us, Josie elbows her twin. Wynona peers through a crack in her black bowl cut. "I guess. Just— if Horatio starts shitting under my ficus tree again…"

"That was one time," I protest.

"And didn't he keep running into my glass walls in the middle of the night?" Wynona recalls, starting to sit up.

"He was recovering from being spayed and was having a bad week," I grumble, already knowing I'm fighting a losing battle.

Calling Horatio well-behaved is like calling a tomato blue: it just doesn't work.

"Hold on." Apparently, contrary to our expectations, Wynona's not drunk enough at all, since she's waxing poetic on poor Horatio's failings. Of which there are, admittedly, a fair amount. "Didn't he jump on my bed in the middle of the night and, for no discernible reason, leave a massive, stinking shit…"

"OK, OK!" I snap. "We've got some work to do on his behavior."

"Work?" Wynona barks out a laugh. "Try Mission Impossible. How many doggy schools and trainers have given you two the boot by now?"

"You were more helpful when you were sobbing over your personal failings," Josie says sweetly.

Wynona grabs the ice cream bowl and then, seeing the pink mush that remains, scowls. "And you were more helpful when you were offering me edible ice cream."

Josie yanks the bowl back and takes a big mushy spoonful with another satisfied blonde eyelash flutter. "You snooze, you lose."

Wynona totters upright. "No, you get sober, you lose. I'm getting a drink."

Two shaky steps and I'm right there beside her. "I'll get this one."

"Well." Wynona draws herself up to her full 5'0" height, still seeming to tower over me even though she's a good head shorter. "Fine."

On my way to the bar, my glance goes to the far table. The long-haired hot guy from before isn't there, but—

Whoa.

Something slams into me.

"Watch where you're going," a deep voice grumbles. It seems so deep that it resonates in my chest, or it could be that I'm still steadying myself on the bar.

"Right back at you," I snap, looking up into narrowed hazel eyes.

Hazel eyes that I've seen before.

Yeah, the long-haired guy is even hotter close up and pissed off. Although he is a jerk.

Ever heard of 'sorry'?

He pauses there, looking me up and down like I'm some sort of art exhibit. His stance is still that annoying combination of ease and tension, of wanting and knowing that he'll get what he wants. He even smells dark and musky.

Jerk.

His mouth opens, then closes. Then, his dark eyebrows drawing together, he turns on his heel and storms off and out of the door.

I stand there for a few seconds, steadying myself on the linoleum countertop of the bar, getting a hold of myself. What the hell just happened?

I can feel the bartender's impatient eyes drilling a hole into my side, but I don't care. I need a second, buddy, OK?

I take a breath, then turn to him. "Two Bloody Marys, please."

Josie's our DD, and I wasn't planning on drinking, but after what just happened, I might be up for a drink. Or two.

Back at the table, Wynona mumbles a pouty thanks as she downs half her drink, while Josie quirks a knowing reddish-blonde eyebrow. "I see you got all up close and personal with one of the hot guys."

"Yeah, more than I could've wanted," I grumble. "Guy was a total jerk."

As I sip my drink, we chat for a few more minutes, trying and failing to cheer Wynona up. Then, out of nowhere, Josie reaches into my bag. "Uh, Sierra?"

I stare at the iPhone 12 Pro she has in her hand blankly. God knows I don't have enough money for that.

As comprehension dawns on me, I rise. "Great. It must've dropped into my purse when we bumped into each other."

I hurry to his table—but all the people there are gone. A quick rush to the door and glance outside finds no sign of him either.

"Guess I have Mystery Jerk guy's phone now..." I tell the twins as I return to our table.

"You say that like it's a bad thing," Wynona says, taking it with a mischievous smile.

"Careful," I joke. "You're holding my month's rent there."

She tilts it, looking carefully as the light hits it.

"Hold on," I say. "What are you..."

"Score," she says next second.

"No way," Josie says, bobbing in her seat so much that her strawberry blonde waves do a little jump too. "It worked?"

Wynona's smile is pure satisfaction, even with half her lipstick missing. "It worked. These rich pricks are all the same—think they're invincible. Don't even have the fingerprint or code locks on their phones. Just have to tilt it and see the fingerprint smears in the light to draw the pattern."

I'm not sure I want to know how she's arrived at this generalization, but anyway, after tapping on the screen a bit, she hands the phone to me. "You can do the honors."

I put the phone on the table, eyeing it uneasily. "I don't know..."

Josie rolls her eyes as she picks up the phone. "We'll just look at the photos, not use his bank information to buy us a vacation to Tahiti. C'mon, Mom."

My arms are crossed across my chest, but I find my firm frown wilting.

"After all," she continues, as she starts scrolling, "if he didn't want people going through his phone, then he should've taken better care of it. And not be such a jerk—ooo!"

Her eyes pop as she shoves out the phone so I can see. "Check this out."

The photo on the phone screen shows the long-haired guy, a beer in each tan hand, on the edge of a turquoise-water white marble infinity pool that belongs more on some luxury island ad than real life.

"Hot damn," Josie murmurs as she scrolls.

'Hot damn' is right. Photo after photo after too-crazy-to-believe photo makes it clear: this guy is clearly living the life. At least, if your definition of 'the life' is girls, booze, and parties—lots of them. That plus a staggering amount of mansion selfies, the odd villa or two, a Porsche that probably costs my entire salary last year—yeah, calling him 'rich' wouldn't be doing his lifestyle justice.

"He looks familiar," Wynona says contemplatively, as she rotates one picture of him riding a camel until it's upside-down.

"Why?" I ask, as she moves on to the next photo and does the same thing: rotate upside-down, then save.

She tilts her head, squints, then nods as she repeats the rotate-save for the next photo. "It'll teach him some manners."

I roll my eyes. "Yeah, because whenever anyone hacks into my phone and saves a bunch of my pictures upside-down I totally rethink my past transgressions."

They're hardly listening.

"You're right, though," Josie's saying, reaching for the phone in vain, as Wynona moves away so she can continue her photo-flipping spree. "Isn't our phone jerk one of the Storm boys? That famous rich family who's in TV or something?"

I lean over to peer at the latest picture Wynona is rotating: the long-haired guy with a bunch of somewhat similar looking guys—brothers? "Hey, I think you're right."

I've never been big on celebrity gossip, but the Storm family is just famous enough for me to have heard of them.

Wynona's sat back in the booth, a wicked smile spreading over her lips, which are losing more black lipstick with every sip of her Bloody Mary.

"Hey," she says. "Know what we should do?"

Josie and I exchange a look: whatever it is, it won't be good.

CHAPTER 3

Nolan

This isn't fucking real.

Yeah, Dad was unpredictable and cagey at his worst, but he wouldn't pull this. Not on me.

Damn it, the old man was a bachelor from the second he left Mom all the way up until the day he died! He wouldn't have...

I pause to lean on my Porsche, cursing as the car alarm shrills into action.

"Fuck's sake," I mutter, jamming the button on my keys.

Even after the alarm shuts up, it still feels like it's going off in my head.

Married... in three months... Married... in three months... Jesus.

"Nolan," Landon calls from behind me.

I swivel around to see the others heading to their cars with sad waves my way, while he strides towards me purposefully.

"I'm sorry," he says, coming to a stop in front of me. If his pockets weren't the stupid sewed-up kind, he'd probably have his hands shoved in them, judging by how they're awkwardly tensed right over the pocket area. Realizing that my own hands are shoved inside my leather jacket, I rip them out, unball them. Sometimes it's funny how Landon and I unconsciously mirror each other. Right now, though, nothing is funny.

I don't want his 'sorry'. I just want tonight swept away, thrown out.

First, the renos are insanely behind, and now this...

Though who am I kidding? 'Now this' is in a league of its own, if I don't get it sorted out. Which I will. There's no way whatever cockeyed nonsense Dad wrote in his will is the last say on this. 'Marry in three months'. What am I in, some B-level romantic comedy destined straight for DVD?

"I don't know what to say," Landon's saying now.

Yep, this is all fucked. Normally, I'm the one saying things. Cracking jokes, filling the silence.

Only the wheelbarrow of my thoughts keeps churning along unsteadily…

Married… in three months… Married… in three months…

No. Fuck no.

"I don't care what Dad wrote," I snarl, feeling for my phone. It's not in my pocket, but this jacket has a shit-ton of pockets—it's bound to be in one of them. "He can't actually expect…"

"No one expects you to actually marry in that time frame," Landon says reasonably.

"No one except Daddy dearest," I mutter, dropping my hands.

I can find my fucking phone later. Right now, I need to get my head around this. Not that I'll be able to, I think.

After all the grief the old man put me through in my teens, I would've thought his last act to me would've been… I don't know, not complete bullshit? Is that too much to ask?

"Hey," I say, eyeing Landon as an idea forms in my head. "How about we pull an old Nolandoner: you impersonate me, pretend that I stole Kyra from you, then marry Kyra, then get the money and…"

Landon's already shaking his head, not that I expected anything different.

"You could've at least pretended to think about it," I grumble.

Landon shrugs. "Waste of time. Listen, I'll just give you half of my portion. It's only fair."

What really would have been fair is if our dear father hadn't royally fucked me over, but who's keeping track?

"Nolan," he repeats.

"I don't want your charity," I snap. "I have my own money."

Problem is, most of it is tied up in the goddamn club, three-quarters of which is closed until who-knows-fucking-when. The quarter we have open is just covering rent and operating costs—barely.

I force my thoughts off the problem at hand to my surroundings.

Manhattan's busy tonight. Taxis and cars zip past, some university girls howl with giggles as one of them recounts a stupid-sounding story. Gasoline fumes from the cars and fast food aromas from the hot dog stand nearby fight to see who will come out on top.

Landon tries to pat me, although his hand is as tense as my shoulder.

"Whatever you need," he says. "I'm here."

I peer at him. "Who are you and what have you done with my brother?"

Landon and I don't do heart-to-hearts, and that's the way I'd like to keep it, thank you very much.

Landon has the decency to at least look rueful.

I let out a low whistle. "Has you well-trained, Kyra does."

He scowls. "It's not like that."

"No?" I round to shoot him a sardonic smirk. "Alright. Come out with me tonight, then. I can get us in Axel, no problem. Get us our old table. Emerson would probably be game to join too."

His scowl deepens. "You know I can't do that."

"Why? Didn't clear it with the wifey first?"

His glare cuts to me. "I have responsibilities now, Nolan. It's not the worst thing in the world, you know."

"No," I say quietly. "But it's sure not the best thing, either."

He stands there, shaking his head. Yeah, yeah, he thinks I don't get it. And he's right. I didn't understand his fixation with Kyra back then, and I still didn't now. Yeah, they had history together and she is hot—but there are tons of hot girls he has history with. Hell, there are tons of hot girls I have history with, and you don't see me sliding a ring on any of them.

Landon's just standing there, probably waiting for me to tell him to fuck off, so he can be done with twin duty.

I glare at the sidewalk, the squiggly crack that has a brave little dandelion poking out of it. "You think I should do it. Go for it. You had some idea he was going to pull this. That's why you've been on my case about this goddamn marriage nonsense. That's why."

It's all making sense now. Hindsight is 20/20. So is my vision, come to think of it. Fuck, I never saw this coming.

Sometimes, when my brother makes an expression I don't recognize and I can't ever remember making myself, it galls me. I have no idea what he's thinking. Like now.

"I didn't know for sure," he confesses. Ah, so that's what it is: guilt. "He made some cryptic comments, but you know Dad. He could swear up and down about something and then never follow through.”

Could and did. There’s a whole bucket list of shit Dad and I never got to—and never will, now. Maybe there’d be room for me to be sad about that if I wasn’t so goddamn angry right now.

Anyway, what’s there to be sad about? Dad lived it up to the very end. Sure, he probably would’ve liked to keep on living it up a little longer, but the man lived to be 72. Not a bad age to go.

And he lived life to the fullest, unencumbered by, say, a goddamn forced marriage stipulation in a will.

Yeah, I’m not the least bit bitter about this. Not one bit.

“Anyway, after Kyra and I got back together,” Landon’s saying now, “I realized that finding someone wasn’t the worst thing.”

I eye him incredulously. Would you look at that half-smile! The fool actually means it. He’s drinking his own Kool-Aid.

“Talk to me when you’ve been together a year, five years, a decade,” I grumble, shaking my head. Whenever reality does finally hit, it’s not going to be pretty. “I’m sure it was all kisses and rainbows the first few months for Mom and Dad too.”

And we know all too well that at the end it was as far from that as you can get without outright beheading the other person.

Landon takes so long to respond that for a minute I don’t think he’s going to at all.

“It wasn’t, actually,” he finally says, a frown forming around the words. “Mom told me one time, before she left. That she always knew. Dad could never seem to keep his eyes or his hands to himself. Yeah, he’d make promises and change for a few months... but it never stuck. Always felt like they were treading water, she said. Avoiding the inevitable."

I glance at him sharply. "She said that to you?"

He looks away. From just the profile view, he looks more like my brother, more like me. I don't have to see the latent happiness and ease that's contoured his face different from mine these past few months.

"She appreciated what you did for her," he says carefully.

"I don't give a shit about that!" I find myself yelling. A middle-aged woman with a big straw hat lowers her massive aviators to give me the full burn of her scandalized gawk.

I glare right back at her. Hello lady? It's fucking nighttime.

Although I do lower my voice as I direct my glare back at my brother. "Just don't try and talk me into the same ploy you and everyone else has fallen for."

"It's not a ploy," Landon says simply.

He's looking at me all sad, the way he looked when he got better shit in his stocking since he had been a good boy and Santa had rewarded him accordingly. Like I was missing out.

When really, he's the one who is. The world's full of women: tall, short, skinny, curvy, busty, bubble-butted, wild, crazy, whatever—and he's shacked up with one for eternity. For the entire one life he has, 'til death do us...

"Whatever can be said for... that." I'm kicking at the sidewalk, even though there's nothing to kick, not even a cigarette butt or stray leaf. "Three months isn't enough time to do it. Dad's rushing me into the same mistake he made: a whirlwind romance ending in utter shit."

Landon says nothing, hands slung in his pockets, face thoughtful. For all the 'utter shit', I guess the case could be made for us making Mom and Dad's relationship somewhat worthwhile. So maybe their relationship wasn't a complete waste, but still.

Or maybe Landon's thinking of a way to get me out of this. Or wondering whether he's stood here and argued with me long enough and can finally go back to his dear Kyra.

I'll do him a solid and be the one to end this.

I grab the car door and pull. "I should go."

Again, that hand on my shoulder. He always did like going into big brother mode, Landon. Even though his big brother status was earned with seconds to spare. "If you need anything…"

I shrug him off. "I need Dad back. And none of this will bullshit." I wheel around to glare it into him. "Think you can do that for me, twinsy?"

He just stands there, eyeing me like he's the one who asked the question.

Someone further down the street yells: a party-goer, a hobo, I'll probably never know.

The point is, the night is young, and I'm not old, not yet. I'm still young enough to enjoy tonight, to make something out of it other than a piss-poor disappointment.

"See ya," I say, and close the door.

I sit there, enjoying the ass-warming leather seats I had to have reupholstered after Jax's crazy goth girlfriend stabbed a knife into it to make a point.

Something's nagging at me and it takes me a few seconds to realize what.

It's the girl.

The one back in the restaurant with the hello body, brown-red hair and blue eyes. The one I later bumped into on my way out. The one who, if it were any other night, I would've chatted up the rest of the night. The one I could still go back to, talk to, take home with me. The one who could maybe save tonight from being a stinking pile of utter shit.

I pause, gazing out the car window. The night is young and full of possibility, but is she the one I want to choose?

One flash of the memory of her in my head and I get out of my seat, heading back to the restaurant. Inside, it's emptier than I remember. Behind the bar, Rodney gives me a nod that means one of those whiskeys he's pouring has my name on it.

But I didn't come here to drink my sorrows away, no. Right now, I plan to drown my sorrows a better way…

A way that's looking increasingly like a long shot. My glare traces the club once, then twice. I see a tableful of glum blonde 40-somethings, another table of obnoxiously happy looking friends, then a recently-vacated spot, but no her.

Fuck it.

No, whatever I hoped, there will be no saving tonight.

Back in my car, cruising home and blasting Metallica, at a stop light, it hits me.

I don't have to take this sitting down. Just because of what some sheet of paper says? Some sheet of paper I didn't even see myself? Not that my brothers would lie about something like that, but still.

I have one of NYC's top lawyers at my disposal, who's paid to find loopholes in legal documents that for any regular old loser would be the kiss of death. That's something.

I drive the rest of the way to my place with less speeding and swerving and passing.

The lobby is empty, Bob the doorman nods officiously, and next thing I know, I'm up in the elevator. Two seconds inside my place, though, and Jax is loping over, a dangerously eager smile on his long-toothed face. "You know what today needs?"

CHAPTER 4

Sierra

"Ughhhh…" I groan blearily against the blinding shaft piercing my eyeballs. "Light."

"Shut up," Josie moans from beside me. "Just… no talking."

Wynona, apparently, is beyond speaking, only has enough stamina to make a low liquidy moan.

"I knew we never should've listened to you and gone to that other club," I grumble at her, staggering for the kitchen. Right now, the only thing that makes any sort of sense is Doritos. As soon as my fingers find purchase on the crackling familiar red bag, I hurtle back to my room and heave onto my bed.

One bite, two… mmmmm… thank the Lord…

"Hallelujah," Josie breathes after the first bite.

"There is a God," I agree quietly, lost in mmm heaven.

We crunch away at the cheesy yumminess for a while more.

"Sierra?" Josie says.

I peer at her, then crack up.

"What?" she says indignantly.

"Look in the mirror," is all I can say between giggles.

Grabbing the chip bag, Josie flounces over to the mirror, then groans. "When did we let Wynona do my makeup?"

I can't stop laughing. Whether Wynona did it from drunkenness or revenge, the result is the same: Josie's eyes are smeared pandas, her lips lined with dark red so crooked and uneven that it looks like a joke.

"When we got back here after you stole my date," Wynona states morosely, reaching between us to grab a chip from the bag.

"You mean the guy who was all over me?" Josie replies smoothly, deftly grabbing the chip out of her fingers.

Wynona grabs it back. "The one who asked for my number, you mean."

I grab the chip and pop it into my mouth. "Guys. We are not going there. Have you forgotten Killian the Almost Irish so soon?"

Scowling, Josie manages to grab a chip, pop it in her mouth and sigh, all at the same time. "Ah, Killian. The Almost Irish."

"Don't remind me," grumbles Wynona, grabbing a handful of chips.

Killian was the Irish dreamboat at our high school with curly red hair, unfairly beautiful cyan blue eyes and a killer sense of humor, who, in Grade 12, almost created an unbridgeable rift between the twins due to his (allegedly innocent) courting of the two. Him mixing up one for the other (and neither correcting him) went on for a good two months until they figured out his game and summarily dumped him. Although he always remained convinced that it was 'the other twin' that dumped him, he—and fighting over a guy—is a mistake the twins have yet to repeat. I'm not about to let them start now.

Finger-combing her strawberry-blonde hair, Josie grimaces at her reflection. "I knew running off to that crazy club right after Wynona said to was a mistake."

"Well, you drinking my drink was your first mistake," Wynona shoots back with her own glare.

"You were toppling over so much they kicked us out," Josie snaps.

Wynona just folds her arms across her chest. "It's called interpretive dance. Look it up."

"Sierra," Josie says through her mouthful of Doritos. "What are you going to do?"

"Well," I say sagely, "I could try putting my TV on craigslist. That should stave off ruin for another week at least."

She swallows with a garbled chuckle. "I meant about the phone."

"Oh." I glance over to see the jerk's fancy IPhonee where I can hazily remember us leaving it on my bedside table. "Guess I can call up the club and return it."

"That would be the ethical thing," Wynona says in a dubious, disapproving voice. "Although… it's probably worth $700, at least."

"I'm not that hard up," I say, frowning at her and picking up my own phone, already Googling the phone number of the comedy club restaurant place.

Wynona must really have a killer headache if she's suggesting I pawn some jerk's phone. For all her tattoos, piercings and old Cary Grant movie pirating, Wynona is such an upstanding citizen that Josie and I have to bully her to even jaywalk with us sometimes.

"Miller Comedy Club and Restaurant on Bank, Rod speaking," a low baritone voice says.

"Yeah, hi," I say. "I've got the phone of someone who bumped into me at your place. Mind if I stop by and drop it off later today?"

"Of course. Hold on."

Muffled voices, then, a minute or so later, there's another voice on the line: "You've got my phone?"

Weird that I'm attracted to a voice—especially when that voice is so frustrated-sounding.

"I think so?" I say coolly. So much for a freaking thank you. "It's an IPhonee 12 Pro?"

"If the case is chrome, that's it."

"It is," I say, turning the chrome-cased phone in my hand. Still waiting on that 'thank you'...

"You'll bring it over now?" is the next thing he says.

My grip tightens on the phone.

Wow. Talk about a tool. Part of me is feeling sorry that I didn't pawn it instead.

"I need it ASAP," he adds, in an even cooler tone.

Who the hell does this guy think I am? His maid?

It takes a good minute of silence before the guy says, "Hello?"

"Yeah, I just woke up," I say, taking his cool tone for myself. Two can play at this game. "I can probably head there in another hour or so."

"That's your definition of ASAP?" he says, his tone light. Although something tells me that his face definitely isn't.

My fists ball. OK, screw this assholey tool. Maybe he's hot and maybe, yeah, we had a moment, but that moment is definitely over. I'm doing him a freaking favor here.

"Oh, sorry," I say sweetly. "You're completely right. Would tomorrow work? Or maybe next weekend? Or you know what? Maybe I could just duct-tape it to my door and you could—"

"In an hour works," he growls.

"Great," I say.

"Great," he says.

I hang up, glaring incredulously at the phone in my hand.

"Told you you should've pawned it," Wynona chimes in helpfully, right before throwing several chips in her mouth.

"I still can," I reply smoothly.

Josie winces. "That bad, huh?"

I nod. "Worse. This guy was acting like he was the one doing me a favor."

"Tool," Wynona grumbles.

"Tool," I agree.

"Tool," Josie agrees.

"You should get his number and sign him up to a bunch of spam call lists," Josie suggests, a mischievous glint in her eyes as she studies her newly panda-eye-free reflection—thanks to liberal use of makeup pads—in my mirror.

"Done," I say, entering the number into my phone.

Who knows, maybe getting spam calls from people claiming to have his social security number and bank information or whatever might humble the guy. Probably not, but at the very least it'll make me feel vindicated. Somewhat.

"You know what you need?" Josie says, starting on her lip balm now. It's a light sparkly hue that only looks good on her—I've tried.

"What?" I say.

She hands me the chip bag.

"You sure?" I say, taking a handful and trying to hand it back to her.

"I'm not," Wynona grumbles, although she makes no move to take the bag.

"Oh, shut up Wyn," Josie says, shoving her with her shoulder before arranging her face into a firm yet kindly smile. "We're sure. Trust me."

After we finish the chips, we have a half-hearted breakfast of some stale Cheerios I'd forgotten I had, then the twins leave. I do a load of dishes, but my heart isn't in it.

"Might as well get this over with," I mutter to myself.

On the car ride there, I have to reject a call from Mom. Probably her updating me about Horatio and checking in about how the job hunt is going. As if she didn't know my prospects so far: a big fat nothing—and as if she wouldn't secretly be pleased about it.

I come out of my reverie at a red light, to find myself glaring so hard at the older lady in the Toyota minivan next to me that she looks downright dismayed. The light changes and I give myself a shake.

Whoops.

I guess the situation is just getting to me. This stupid phone thing, but more than that, my job situation.

Mom wants me to do well, yeah, but she doesn't think I can unless it's on her terms, according to her definition of the world. I can almost hear her voice echoing in my head now: "Life is hard and unsteady. Get a nice, boring job that you hate, but pays the bills". That's what she did: a nine-to-five office management position that has her taking her first glass of wine minutes after getting home and her fifth right before bed. Not that I can really blame her, after what she went through before, but still.

She needs to get that I'm not her.

And I'm not Peyton either: stellar child and life-liver extraordinaire with her perfect job, perfect boyfriend, perfect little Pomeranian. I sound jealous because I am. It doesn't help that, for whatever reason, despite eclipsing me in basically every way possible, Peyton still takes it upon herself to compete with me in basically everything, and make passive-aggressive comments the rest of the time. At least we haven't been talking for the past few months—one problem off my back.

At any rate, here I am again at the boxy red-brick structure where we had dinner last night. All I have to do is drop this stupid phone off—with any luck the jerk was just at the club by chance and won't be here now—go home, and get job hunting. By now, I've lost track of how many versions of my resume I've dropped off and sent off, and to how many places, but the first number would hover around 10 and the second around 250.

At the door, I pause. My car is one of the few in the lot that isn't a pickup truck. Clearly this is before their opening hours, but will the front door even be open?

I give myself a determined nod. The guy on the phone said I could drop by. Besides, I fought the mid-morning traffic (who am I kidding, there's always traffic in NYC) to get here. I am not going away empty-handed. Rather, I am going away empty-handed—I'm getting rid of this goddamn phone so I never have to speak to or set eyes on that jerk again.

One foot inside and I'm pausing again. As far as I can see, the stucco-walled interior looks like dead city, but screw it, I'm going in.

As I open the second set of doors, the shrill of power tools from further in echoes over. Must be from the renovations in the back.

I give the air an experimental sniff, trying to place what it is that I'm smelling. It even seems to smell construction-y in here too, though that could be my imagination.

"Hey," a voice cuts through my daze. "You've got my phone."

Him.

Shit.

So much for avoiding the jerk. He's striding towards me, and yeah, jerk or not, my memory clearly didn't do him justice. Sculpted body, powerful arms, chiseled jaw, rugged eyes with a glint that's slightly sardonic—'hot' doesn't even begin to cover it.

Hello, Earth to Sierra: Speak!

"Hey." My voice comes out a croak, so I swallow, force my hand into my pocket then out, and hand over the phone. "Yeah."

He takes it, our fingers brushing. Electricity ripples from where the slight contact happened.

He's a jerk, Sierra. A complete, impolite, self-absorbed—

"Thanks," he says, standing there.

OK, maybe not a complete jerk. But still, mostly a jerk. One that I should be getting away from stat.

"Right, well, glad to help." Am I the only one thinking I'm sounding like some babbling schoolgirl? Maybe it's because I can't remember the last time I was so close to a guy this hot—maybe never? "I should be going now."

I don't expect any response, and I don't get one. Clearly, whatever 'moment' I thought we had before was in my head.

I head for the door.

"Hey," he says.

I pause.

"Sorry about before," he continues. "I've just had the most insane last 24 hours."

Is he actually… turning to eye him finds that he actually does look sorry. A bit.

Hmm. Maybe not a complete jerk after all.

"I'm Nolan," he says, with a half-smirk indicating that he's pretty damn pleased with himself.

Yeah, this guy oozes douche, though he is hot. OK, like 70% jerk, then.

"Sierra," I say.

"Sierra," he says, half-contemplatively, a slight tilt to his head. As if he likes the taste of my name on his lips.

Nolan, hmm. Do I like the taste of his?

Whoa there, girl. Clearly, I haven't some good one-on-one time with my vibrator for far, far too long.

"Let me make it up to you," he's saying now, an odd light in his eyes. "The favor you did for me."

Oh, so now he's calling it a favor.

Although I can't say that this 'making it up to me' sounds as crappy as it probably should. Maybe Nolan's only, like, 60% jerk, anyway.

Somehow, in the harsh fluorescent glare of the lights overhead, he manages to look both intense and relaxed at once, like a cougar lounging as it hunts its prey. Those hazel questions of his eyes are so mesmerizing that it takes a few seconds for what he said to hit.

Holy hell-cow, is he actually suggesting what I think he is?

And am I actually open to it?

"Hey boss," a beefy looking bald guy says, striding in the room. "Just wanted to let you know, the bathroom layout is all wrong. I know we thought that we'd gotten rid of all Gerard's fuck-ups, but it looks like not. What do you want us to do? They'd already started applying the floor tiles when they realized it."

"Shit." Nolan scowls, eyes enraged slits as he shakes his head. "No one noticed?" He takes a step for the back door, already shaking his head. "I'll go have a look now."

"No need." The bald guy makes a face as he heaves a heavy sigh. "I can tell you right now, the place looks like shit. Since Gerard's measurements were all wrong, the remaining tiles won't even fit properly."

"I thought you said you double-checked everything else," Nolan says, arms crossed over his chest as he glares at the guy. His face is strained between stifled rage and twisted calm. "That's what you told me."

"Nope." The bald guy's pudgy oval of a face assumes a mulish expression. "Told you I double-checked everything else in the main room. All those measurements are A-OK."

"Would logic not suggest you check the entire layout?" Nolan's voice is quiet, contained, yet still vibrating with rage. It's actually kind of hot.

Jesus, what the hell is wrong with me?

At any rate, clearly, Nolan's at least 80% jerk, and judging by the way he and the bald guy are squaring off, has completely forgotten about me. So much for moment #2.

There's only one thing to do. I head for the door and leave. On the way to my car, I almost pause and turn back half-a-dozen times.

I mean, I never even said goodbye, gave Nolan a chance to, I don't know, prove that he meant what he said. That the look in his eyes wasn't just a look. But, as I sit in the traffic that's crawling me back home, if I'm being completely honest with myself, the interruption was just my excuse to leave. Part of me wanted to run away the second we locked eyes.

Maybe there's times when it's good to have an ill-advised, head-over-heels fling with some guy too attractive to believe, but now isn't one of those times. At least not for me.

I have my job situation to worry about, I'm one missed rent payment away from getting the boot, I'm reduced to Googling 'creative ramen recipes'. Now is not the time for me to be going and having a fling with a guy I'm possibly more attracted to than any other, ever.

Especially not knowing what happened the last time I got in way too deep.

Even if, yes, just being around him is like three shots of vodka and yes, he is hot and in control and pure man and—Stop, Sierra.

So, I do. I go home, apply to five more journalist positions I'll never get, and then, after a meal of ramen à la chili (basically, ramen doused with enough chili that I almost like it), Josie calls me up.

"How'd it go?" she asks.

"Which?" I say. "Giving the jerk back his fancy phone, or my never-ending job hunt?"

She chuckles sympathetically. "I guess you answered both questions?"

"He actually wasn't as much of a jerk the second time," I admit. "He even apologized. Apparently, he'd been having a bad day or something."

"Oooh, and?" Josie says.

"No 'and'," I say, frowning. I shouldn't have brought it up, really. What's done is done. "He had to talk to some contractor guy and I left."

"Oh," she says, clearly disappointed.

"Anyway," I say. "Enough about me. How are things with you? Is Wynona feeling better?"

"Not really," she confesses. Movement and shuffling sounds in the background. "Me, I'm just finishing up at work at the nursery here. Some genius knocked over our monstera, and I get to shovel all the dirt back into the pot." A self-conscious chuckle, then a grunt of exertion. "OK, maybe I'm just bitching for the sake of it. I actually don't mind repotting and all that. It's soothing."

"Maybe I should try it," I quip. "Do you think Wynona needs a Round Two?"

"Maybe," Josie says. Then a grunt. "Dear sweet Lord Jesus, that's a heavy boy. I mean it, Sierra, you need to stop by sometime to see how big this guy has gotten."

"I was just there two months ago," I remind her.

"Two months for a fast-growing plant with a grow light and fertilizer is like two human years," Josie informs me officiously. "Anyway, while Wynona might need to do shots until the world is spinning and she barfs out all her relationship trauma, I, on the other hand, am not sure I can tolerate another last night so soon. My head is still pounding, although maybe it's the four Advils I popped."

"Four?" I almost yell. "Josie, I told you, I did a research paper on them, and—"

"I know, blah blah blah, health concerns, blah," she grumbles. "Can we just focus on Wynona how we were before?"

"Fine," I say grudgingly. "Anyway, what about a girls' night tonight? We can watch one of the Scary Movies, and I can pick up some charcoal face masks too."

"Ooooh," Josie says. "Those the ones that hurt?"

"You betcha," I say, wincing even as I smile at the thought. I actually heard of them first from Peyton, before we stopped talking. "The ones that rip all your gross blackheads out. Our pain is our skin's gain."

"Count me in," Josie says, even though her skin is flawless enough to be used in a skin cream ad. "And Wynona too. She could do with some pain that's not in her heart."

"I'll get her her own Doritos bag too," I suggest.

"Yeah," Josie says. "You do that. I'll get her there. She was muttering about feeling sick today, but we both know it's because she had the brilliant idea to have Fuzzy Peaches for lunch and an eggnog after that."

We chuckle.

"Alright," I say, feeling better already. Being around the twins has that effect on me. "I'll head out and pick up those masks. See you at eight?"

"Holddddd up," Josie cuts in. "How about Wynona picks up the masks? She's got enough money to buy us a charcoal mask factory, after all."

"Josie," I grumble. I know where this is going, and I don't like it. "They're, like, three dollars each. And the pharmacy is across the street from me."

"I know, but..."

"Josie!" I snap. "I'm not poor!"

I exhale. "OK, I am poor, for now. But I can still afford stupid charcoal masks."

"OK," Josie says, a defensive edge to her voice. If she were here, she'd be throwing up her sparkly colorful-nailed hands. "Just trying to help."

"I know, and I appreciate it, I'm just..." I'm not sure what the word is, but I settle on "stressed, is all."

"And I told you, anytime you want to head over to the nursery while I'm here, and—"

"Sorry, but digging through the wormy dirt and hoping that whatever new pot I plop the plant into doesn't kill it isn't my idea of relaxing," I say drily.

Josie sighs. "OK, fair enough. Well. Your birthday is coming up and that new spa is almost open, so..."

"That might be more up my alley," I admit, my smile forming around the words. "Now, gotta go! The lines at the pharmacy get insane around 4:30, and I don't want to wait while some crazy person argues with the cashier over the price of gum."

Josie chuckles. "See ya."

"See ya."

I get to the pharmacy just in time to avoid the rush, although I do encounter a grumpy teenage cashier with hair bleached within an inch of its life who is so done with work. So done with work that she somehow manages to ring the masks in at a dollar apiece and, when I point out her mistake, just shrugs with a promising "Whatever."

So I get three masks for the price of one and head back to my place thinking that today might not be so bad after all. All I need is the tiniest, slightest hint of an actual interview, and then…

Just like that, he comes back into my head.

Six foot something tall, broad shoulders. A smirk that knows what it wants.

Let me make it up to you…

And me, answering in my head what I never did in person: Don't mind if you do.

I give myself a little shake. If I'm going on mental excursions to la-la what-if land, it's clearly time for me to do a pre-friend clean of my place. Which includes moving my laptop away from the couch and arranging the chip bags in a line.

There. Done.

The twins arrive a little under an hour later. Wynona, sure enough, looks about as glum as last night before we went drinking.

"He texted me," she says lugubriously, after finishing her first glass of wine and starting on her second. "Wants me to stop texting him."

"Huh?" I say. "But wasn't he the one who texted you?"

Her eyebrows leap as her blue eyes assume a fearsome expression. "He plays mind games, Sierra. Mind games." Another sip. "Men. They rip out your heart and blame you for bleeding on the floor."

I push the Dorito bag a bit closer to my friend as I eye her pensively. "Ever consider becoming a poet, Wynona?"

We all crack up at that.

"You should've heard her rap Edgar Allan Poe's 'The Raven' back in tenth grade English," Josie says, looking up, hand flying to her chest as she shakes her head with delight. "Standing ovation, that got. Glorious, it was."

"Glad my pain is so amusing to you two," Wynona comments drily, although she's smiling as she reaches for a chip.

"I think this calls for some face masks," I say, rising.

Josie gulps. She knows what's in store for us. "It's time?"

I nod. "It's time."

An hour of mask time and watching Scary Movie later, my phone alarm goes off.

"Now, it's really time," I say, grinning.

"We couldn't wait until..." Josie trails off, knowing that it's hopeless. We're going to have to take off these masks eventually. Not that I blame her for trying to put it off a bit longer. She's basically a wimp when it comes to pain.

"Let's get this over with," Wynona says glumly.

She's hardly laughed at any of the jokes in Scary Movie 3, and her mouth has hardly changed from that twisted frown, like she ate something rotten and has to deal with it.

Minutes later, we rip off the masks, squealing and laughing our heads off at how red yet gloriously baby-smooth our skin underneath is. At least, Josie and I do. Wynona just stands there, glaring at her reflection like it's to blame for her current pain. Which I guess, in a way, it is.

Apparently, with Jeremy, the word 'soulmate' was tossed around. Apparently, he even had their wedding spot picked and everything.

The same weekend he cheated on her with some stripper he'd met at... you guessed it, a strip club. A strip club he'd apparently been a regular at.

Jesus, men can be animals. People can be, really, but what this guy did to my friend makes me want to...

"Hey," Josie says softly, leaning over to give her a side-squeeze. "Your skin looks really good."

"Wonderful," Wynona says with no emotion. Then she sighs. "Sorry for being such a downer, guys. Maybe I should just go."

"No!" I protest. "I didn't even tell you about..."

I trail off, trying to think of what exactly I haven't told her about since the 12 or so hours ago I saw her last.

"Your meet-up with super-hot jerk," Josie provides.

"Oh, right." I press my lips together. Not exactly the topic I'd choose, but Wynona has perked up with interest, so I guess that's something. "Yeah, so I went to see him, and surprise, surprise, he was still a jerk."

A pretty succinct summary, but I'm not really eager to recount our meeting. Already, there's a weird feeling in my stomach, and I'm replaying the final scene in my mind, me staying, asking: "Hey. Did you mean what you said about making it up to me?"

"That's not all," Josie points out. "You said he wasn't as much of a jerk. And he apologized."

"And offered to make it up to me," I blurt out before I can stop myself.

Sierra. You stupid, stupid woman.

"What?!?" Josie says, spraying wine she's so surprised. "You definitely didn't mention that. You've been holding out on me!"

"For like a couple hours," I mumble. "Anyway, it wasn't a big deal. He ended up getting in this argument with some contractor guy, and I just left."

"Without saying goodbye?" Josie says, frowning at me, though she already knows the answer.

"Sorry, Mom," I grumble back. "I wasn't about to stand around waiting for some jerk to remember I'm there."

"Come off it," Wynona chimes in. "You ran away."

"I did not," I protest, cheeks heating up.

"You did so," Josie says, shaking her head and tut-tutting. "Come on, Sie, we know you. Remember what you did for prom when Eric asked you?"

"I... just had to check something," I mutter.

"You run away when you like a guy." Wynona strokes the length of her nose, evidently amused by its post-mask smoothness. "Admit it."

"OK." I stand up. "I don't know when the topic switched to me and my love life—or lack thereof—but I don't like it."

"You're right." Wynona visibly deflates in her seat, apparently remembering she had some chips in her mouth as she starts chewing. "We should continue on with my poor life choices."

"Hey now," Josie protests with a wagging finger. In the matter of a day, she's switched her nail shade to bright yellow and orange. "No one ever said you make poor life choices."

Wynona rises. "Well, you're both thinking it."

"No, we're not," I say, rising too. "Wyn, none of us really has it together, OK?" I stand there, feeling so useless. I want to hug her, tell her I love her, tell her that I know she'll find a guy who doesn't treat her like trash, a guy who recognizes how amazing she is. But I also want to tell her to stop choosing assholes. So, I just sit there and babble out something else: "Want to know what would be a poor life choice? Me texting that guy."

"You do have his number," Josie says, leaning forward in her seat as eagerness kindles in her blue eyes. "Though I disagree about the classification part."

Wynona's already sunk back into her gloom, though, judging by the slump of her shoulders and the curve of her lips. We'll need to rustle her out of it fast—if we're going to be able to at all.

I take out my phone, open up the camera application, and give it my ugliest, creepiest smile, complete with bulging psycho-looking eyes, before taking a picture. I glance at the twins, all of us chuckling as I turn the phone their way. "Maybe I should send him that?"

"No caption, just that picture." Josie laughs so much she snorts as she looks at the hideous result. "Perfect."

Even Wynona cracks a smile as she looks at it, although she shakes her head. "You need something more sexy, less ugly."

We both know I'm never going to send any of these, but I giggle as I unzip my hoodie to play along. Anything to make my friend smile. "OK, boss."

"Oh yeah, girl!" Josie cheers, giggling away. I position my cleavage, then give the camera my most sultry face at the same time I give it the finger. When I check the result, I end up staring at it for a good few seconds.

"What?" Josie says. "Come on, show us!"

"It's..."

Well, what's the word? Sexy? I don't know, I've never been big on taking 'those' sort of photos—I've always been too paranoid that they'd be leaked. After all, it happened to one girl in our school back in 11th grade—Erin, wasn't it?—and she never got over it. Apparently, it even fucked up her university applications and she now works at some sort of call center trying to scam people out of their old air conditioners or something.

But now that I'm looking at the picture—me, with the smile that came from I don't know where, my bare breasts pressed into a hot V of cleavage—I can see where the allure comes from. I look good. I look damn good.

"Ooooh," Josie squeals as she peers over to see the picture. Then she laughs. "Love the middle finger."

"What can I say," I say in a faux haute couture voice. "I'm model material."

"Let me see," Wynona protests.

When I hand her the phone, her eyes light up. "Wow." She taps away.

"Hey," I say. "What are you…"

I grab the phone just in time to see the SENT signature on the photo she just sent to 1-718-675-3434. AKA Nolan's number.

I sit there, staring at it in sheer shock for a few seconds. When I can finally speak, all I can say is: "You didn't."

CHAPTER 5

Nolan

"Found anyone to marry yet?" Jax teases.

I toss a striped Kleenex box that misses him by an inch, thanks to his quick ducking.

"Bro," he grumbles.

"Aren't you supposed to be a dodgeball whiz?" I ask innocently.

He scowls bigger, and I regret it. Even if Jax pressed my buttons first. He can't help it—the man loves a good argument the way rabbits love carrots. He's a good guy in spite of that.

And in spite of him ordering about five boxes of pizza after I came home from the dinner last night, and eating four.

Right now, I basically feel like shit. Earlier today, after some more unproductive time at the comedy club trying to get the renos into something other than a complete fiasco, I tried calling up Dirk. After hours of him dodging my calls, he finally answered, long enough to say that no, there was no way around my Dad's will stipulation and yeah, basically I was screwed. OK, maybe not the second part, but it pretty much came down to that, close enough.

Slinging himself on the couch next to me, Jax repeats, "So, you find your honey yet?"

I gesture to the pizza box on one side of me, the thong of whatever girl stayed over a few nights ago on the other. "What does it look like?"

Jax dangles the thong from his finger, gives it a little whirl, then tosses it off. "Maybe she's right under your nose and you've been missing her?"

"And maybe you need to fuck off," I grumble. I open the pizza lid to find one sad excuse for a slice that I take anyway. Maybe food will make me feel less pissed off.

Although part of me being pissed off is that I'm pissed off in the first place. Why should I give half a shit about some chick who showed up, gave me my phone back, then disappeared before I could even ask for her number?

There's at least four billion women in the world, at least a quarter of those eligible, last time I checked.

"Speaking of honeys," I say, mouth full of pizza. "Won't Laura be worried about where you are? You've been here, what, like four days now?"

Jax gives a wiggly sort of shrug / head-shake.

"Well?" I say, giving him my most winning smile.

His scowl darkens, then sags. "Just don't tell her I'm here. Please?"

I sigh, enjoying the last of the olive-pepper pizza. It really was good, but small. "What was it this time?"

His jaw tenses. "I hooked up with her sister."

"Dude," I say, having to laugh.

"Well, I didn't know it was her sister, now did I?" Jax says, arms crossed over his chest defensively. "I mean, she looked kind of familiar, but... hey!"

"Sorry," I say, though I still can't stop laughing. "But dude."

"I know, dude, I know. They aren't on speaking terms, so maybe she won't find out, but—"

"At the risk of repeating myself, why not break up with her?"

Jax just shakes his head sagely. "You know I can't do that."

I give him my most shit-eating grin. "I think 'won't' is the word you were looking for there."

When he doesn't answer, I continue, "C'mon, man. You broke up with her in the first place because you caught her cheating on you, remember? Several times with the same guy, and even a few times with another couple of guys. And that's not counting the time she keyed your car because you forgot to post a birthday greeting on her Facebook wall after you threw her that big surprise party. Or the time she dropped your dog off at your aunt's and told her you didn't want it anymore because it barked too much. Or the time she crashed your car and wouldn't pay to have it fixed. Need I go on?"

The answer is implicit in the question, but Jax just shakes his light curly-haired head and keeps on shaking it. "You don't understand, man."

"You're right." I shrug as I get up, heading for the fridge. There's bound to be something decent in there. I hope. "And I sure as hell don't want to."

If I needed any more convincing about the shit-show relationships turn out to be, after seeing Mom and Dad, then I'd just need to look at Jax and his more off-then-on-again girlfriend, the demon who calls herself 'Laura'. The woman's a class-A psycho who will probably end up in jail for murder and/or assault, but for some mysterious reason Jax never seems to be able to voice, he won't leave the nutjob.

"Anyway," Jax says now, just as my phone goes off, his lips peeling back in a horrified grimace at what he says next. "I should head over there. Throw myself on her mercy."

"Ahhh... don't think that's a good idea," I say, trying to keep my voice light.

The poor man looks like he's going to topple over as it is.

He just shakes his head. "It's the right thing to do."

Yeah, 'right' if you want an early grave, and/or a premature heart attack, I think.

"Maybe she'll understand?" I say instead.

Now isn't the time to bring up the time she went on a Facebook deleting spree, deleting every female on Jax's Facebook (including Jax's grandma, who was using a pseudonym and a picture of an ombre sunset instead of her face), just because she caught him talking to some female she didn't recognize on it (it was actually an event organizer for a cancer awareness fundraiser he was planning to attend, which she later refused to believe).

Not that I can blame Laura for being paranoid. Jax is a catch. Other than him liking to push his close friend's buttons the odd time, he's as good as they come: handsome, a basketball player—although he's currently off for an injury—the man even volunteers every week and helps teach basketball at our local YMCA. If that's not enough, my boy has dimples, which I wouldn't have thought was a thing, except every other girl who I've banged and has met him has delightedly brought it up. Huh.

"See ya," Jax says, at the door now.

"Good luck," I call, though he's already out the door and he needs something more than luck.

Nothing less than divine intervention will do for my unfortunate lovesick friend. Except at this point, I'd venture to say that this isn't love. This is cancer.

I sigh.

Odds are, I'll be seeing him later tonight, if he is still even alive. Not that I'm overly worried. While Laura has been known to throw the odd brand-new $500 Vitamix blender or $4,000 Apple laptop, she's five foot nothing, 90 pounds, and basically has no decent knives on hand since she eats takeout exclusively.

Jax has been staying at my place every few weeks for the past year because that's how often he and Laura have another blow-up. I don't mind the company, and he throws good parties. Plus, we've been friends since we were kids. Plus, when he parties, he's hilariously crazy.

My stomach gives a whining roar, and I switch my focus over to the fridge.

Huh.

I've got mustard, ketchup, relish, sriracha, mayonnaise, salsa, steak sauce and one single moldy tomato.

"Goddammit," I mutter.

I guess Pizza Pizza it is. I go over to my phone and, clicking open the latest message, hold it. And hold it.

What in the hell...

Out of all the messages I could've expected to see, this would come dead last on the list. Hell, I'd expect to get a message from Jax that he'd just gotten torpedoed en route to Laura's by none other than Laura herself, in cahoots with some Russian extremists, before getting this.

Hello there.

Brown-red hair rumpled, a teasing beckon of a smile... As if the rest wasn't enough... her breasts squeezed together begging for me to put my hand between them and enjoy their fullness myself.

Oh fuck.

Hard from a fucking picture? What am I, twelve?

That, plus... the middle finger.

I find a smile curving on my face too. I like this girl already.

Food forgotten, I shoot off a text: Hello to you too.

Nothing. I Google Pizza Pizza and am about to dial their number when—

—Didn't mean to send that.

I can pretend I didn't see it?

—Please do.

OK... What about that date?

A pause that's too long. I grab the pizza box and walk over to chuck it into the recycle bin. By the time I get back, she's responded: What date?

The one I was going to take you on before you ran off.

—Didn't seem like you'd be done with your business anytime soon.

OK, well. I'm sorry. Now I have two things to make it up to you, so, let's say one amazing date?

I scowl at her lack of response. Clearly, the woman likes keeping me hanging. Too bad I'm not about to give up that easily. I've suddenly got one of my killer ideas, one that'll solve the twin problems of my gnawing hunger and wanting to see her ASAP.

Willow. Meet me there in an hour?

—I have plans.

Two hours? Tomorrow?

Maybe I'm moving too fast. Usually I regale the girls with some good old Nolan original texting. I've even helped Emerson from time to time.

Thing is, I want to see her now.

Am I allowed to ask what plans? I text her.

—Do you care?

I chuckle. This girl's got fire, I'll give her that.

Just trying to be polite.

—You weren't so concerned before.

Yep, lots and lots and lots of fire. Not enough to cook me, though. I like it hot.

Listen. I really had a shitty last 24 hours. I'll explain when we meet in person.

—That's fair. I have some friends over. We're watching Scary Movie 3.

One of my favorites. Apparently Simon Cowell regrets being in it though.

—Ha, really? But his scene was so funny!

Agreed. He stopped by my club one time and was grumbling about it. Otherwise, he was super cool though.

Shit, I don't normally feel the need to name-drop. This woman's keeping me on my toes. Fuck. This is why I just need to see her and get it over with. I've never been a patient man.

Tomorrow, then. Eight PM at Willow?

—Sure. Got to go.

Enjoy your movie. Talk later ;)

I stare at my phone. Will we, though? I have the date set up, why bother? Then again, a bit more banter wouldn't hurt.

First, though, a man's gotta have some fuel. I'm going to need a pizza.

My belly rumbles. Make that two.

CHAPTER 6

Sierra

"I'm going to kill you," I tell Wynona before restarting the movie.

"You mean 'you're welcome'?" she shoots back with a sugary sweet smirk on her ruby-red lips, grabbing the remote and pausing the movie again.

"You are not going to just leave us hanging like that!" Josie declares with a dismayed frown, yanking away the wine bottle I'm reaching for.

"Why not?" I ask. "After that stunt Wynona pulled, let's just say I did some damage control."

"I did you a favor," Wynona says stubbornly, tilting up her chin. "You never would've texted the man otherwise."

"A favor?!?" I protest. "Sending that pic when you had no right to, to the last person I'd want to receive it? You couldn't have just—I don't know—sent him a 'hey' text if you really absolutely had to intervene?!?"

"OK, fine," she relents, with a shrug that ends with her shoulders slumping. She wraps her black bat cardigan arms across her chest. "I'm sorry. I'm an awful person, OK? An awful person who just made another shitty life choice."

"Oh stop," I grumble, grabbing the wine bottle and shoving it to her. I feel like wrapping my own arms across my chest. Or just disappearing into a hole in the floor. Or going to that date. Agh! "A simple 'sorry' would've sufficed."

"So you're really not going to tell us," Josie says with a pout.

"Fine." I sigh, shoving as many chips as I can fit into my mouth. I still feel light-headed from our text conversation, as quick as it was. Like I'm riding in a couch pulled by flying horses through clouds… Or, more likely, like I'm a complete idiot. "We're going to Willow tomorrow night."

"AHHH!" Josie says, leaping up and dropping the chip bag.

As Wynona grins and I eye her, she sits back down, picking a piece of lint off her pink cowl-neck sweater, clearly embarrassed. "OK, minor overreaction. But seriously, Sierra, when was the last time you went on a nice date with someone actually promising?"

"He's not promising," I argue. "He's a jerk, remember?"

"A gorgeous rich jerk," Wynona says in an awe-laced voice as she tilts her head to the side.

"Anyway," I continue. "That doctor was OK."

"That doctor was a cheap ass," Josie reminds me firmly, eyes narrowing more with every word. "Remember? He tried pressuring you into coming to his place, then, when that failed, insisted that the only thing he was willing to do otherwise was take a walk in his giant garden."

"It was a nice garden," I recall, trying to smile and failing. Edward, that's what his name was. The creep. "Had lots of these nice flowery shrubs. Though him trying to yank me into his house put a damper on it all. But anyway, I haven't been dating that much lately."

"And it is just a first date," Josie points out, evidently having come to her senses. "He might turn out to be a mega jerk anyway."

"True," Wynona says, not without adding, "A gorgeous rich jerk."

"OK, OK," I say. "Can we watch the movie now? Please?"

"Movie away," Wynona says, pressing the start button.

It only takes a minute before we're laughing again.

That night, after the twins have gone home, I'm about to get into bed when my phone goes off.

It's him: How was the movie?

Good, I text back, then pause. As much as part of me wants to ask him how his night was, and just make idle chitchat, I'm mostly just tired. About to go to bed now.

—What a coincidence, same here! Your bed have a mattress too?

I chuckle, then type: God, we're so alike.

—Don't tell me… you have five fingers too?

Actually, there was an accident and…

—Shit. Sorry. Way to screw up the evening.

Just kidding.

—You wicked, wicked woman. Although I can't say I'm all that good myself.

I find a reluctant smile curving on my lips. Something about this man…

Another text pings:

—Scared you away already?

I bite at my lower lip.

Damn it, why am I getting flustered over some stupid texting, anyway?

I force myself to type out my response, the first thing that comes to mind: Not yet. Guess we'll have to see about that.

—Guess we will. Goodnight Sierra.

Goodnight Nolan.

As I lie there in my bed, despite my fervent wish for sleep, my mind plays out what we would've said if I hadn't mentioned sleep, where the conversation would've gone.

And even though I'm all set to not be able to pay rent on time once again, and there's pills on my old sheets so big my cracked heel catches on them, I find myself smiling.

It's only when I wake up that I realize it: I slept with my phone under my pillow. Like Nolan Storm's a special wish I hope some fairy will grant me.

Ridiculous.

As I chow down ramen à la carte for breakfast, a knock on the door has me heading to it.

"Here's the baby," Mom coos as she sets down Horatio, his gray short-haired form wriggling uncooperatively until all his four paws are on the ground. "He was so good. Only peed on my favorite carpet a few times." She smiles valiantly and I groan.

"I thought, after last time... I'm so sorry."

"Don't be sorry." Mom crouches to give Horatio an affectionate little pat before he trots off, probably in search of some food—or some more mischief he can cause. "It gave me something to do."

"I can buy you a new one?"

"That your way of saying you'll take that IT position that's still on the table? Your uncle says that if you ever change your mind—"

"Mom," I say. "I just mastered the use of Gmail, OK? I'm not sure IT is really up my alley."

"You're a fast learner."

"And in this case, I'd be an unwilling learner."

"Honey," she says, shaking her head sadly as she eyes me, "when are you going to get out of this phase?"

I take a step back, shaking my head too.

I love my mom, but she's never going to let this go.

"How about never? This isn't a phase, Mom, it's my life. I love journalism, and that's what I'm going to do."

Seeing that arguing anymore is useless, Mom finally lets it go, though she sure doesn't look happy about it.

"Want to come in?" I offer.

I feel bad shutting Mom down like I just did. But she never misses a chance to bring it up. It's not like I don't have enough to worry about.

But Mom's already shaking her head. "I'd love to, but I have plans. Brunch with your sister at Beckta, if you…"

"Sorry," I say quickly, before she can finish that very unappealing sentence. "I just ate."

Mom tucks a gray strand behind her ear with a frown. "They do have coffee and tea there, you know. Stuff like that. My treat."

I avoid meeting her gaze. "I really ought to get job hunting."

She touches my arm. "Honey."

I shrug her off. "Don't push it, Mom."

She sighs, both arms falling at her sides. "But you two are my babies. It just makes sense that I'd want you two to get along. Can't you?"

"No." I put more force in the word than I'm feeling. Really, it's just too early for this. And my head's still messed up from the other night and this upcoming maybe-actually-decent date on the table.

Not that I'm ever in the mood to talk about Peyton. "Mom, you know how she is."

The resigned tilt to Mom's blue eyes indicates that she knows full well how she is, but instead, she says, "She's just high-strung, and likes to talk about herself, and…"

"Mom." I don't even bother to let her finish; we both know what she's going to say. She's not going to get me to go along with her doomed peacemaking attempts this time. "Last time I saw her, she went on a 20-minute spiel about her new $1,000 Louis Vuitton shoes before asking me why my sneakers looked so horrid and holey. She's a"—I swallow back the word 'bitch', hearing Mom's scolding tone in my head and quickly replace it with "jerk."

"Well," Mom says firmly. "She's your sister and you should love her."

"Wrong," I reply. "It's even harder because she is my sister. Maybe if she was just an acquaintance, I would know her so little that I'd actually think she was OK. But Mom, she broke half my toys when we were kids, and now that we're adults, she spends most of her time trying to talk down to me or just act superior."

"You know she's just insecure," Mom argues.

"No." I go to the door and open it. "I know that you coddle her and won't accept my decision to stay as far away from her as I possibly can. Anyway, I hope you have a good time."

"Fine," Mom says tersely, heading out the door. "This isn't over."

After the door closes, a sad smile comes over my face. "No. It never will be."

I turn to Horatio, who's studying me carefully. Probably trying to figure out if I'll spoil him as much as Mom did the past few days, to which the answer is: hell no. Mom buys whole organic grain-fed juice-glistening BBQ chickens for the fat little guy.

I do get out his food, water, and his favorite treat, giving him a little pat.

He lets out a low whine, his sleek gray head bowing glumly.

"I know," I say, partially to him, partially to myself. "Things don't always turn out how we'd like."

Although that doesn't mean tonight won't.

The rest of the day is job-searching and ramen-snacking. And then, the text comes:

Tonight at 7 works if I pick you up?

I text back: Sounds good. I'm at 2387 Clair Creek Blvd.

A few minutes later, as I send out resumes that I'm 89% sure won't be responded to, I find myself smiling.

6:30 comes fast and slow, the way it does on days when you have something to look forward to but work to slog through as well.

One minute, I'm shooting off my latest resume, the next I'm standing barefoot in front of my closet an hour before my date, totally stumped.

Horatio pads by to give me a baleful look—he probably just found that I replaced his favorite sheepskin rug that he liked to poop on with a less-appealing scratchy straw one.

My hands paw through the clothes in my closet—mostly Mom's purchases of work-appropriate clothes for the high-flying not-journalism job I still don't have—before returning to my phone.

There's only one thing to do...

"Hello," Josie says, picking up. "Last-minute date SOS?"

"Yeah," I admit. "I have no clue what to wear."

"Still deciding between classy or slutty?" she says knowingly, and I can pretty much hear her devilish smile over the line.

"I can't be both?" I joke, then sigh. "Honestly, yes. I feel nervous and hungry enough that maybe my uncomfortable dresses aren't a good idea, and I'm pretty sure that one dress makes me look like a pregnant murderess and—"

"Accept my video request," Josie says succinctly.

"Fine," I say, turning on my video.

"Now, try on a few, and I'll give my verdict," she says sternly, face matching her tone. "Don't you have a few from your aunt you could try?"

"Believe me," I tell her. "We do not want to go there."

"Retro can be cool," she argues, and once again I can practically see the stubborn set of her probably coral-glossed lips from just her tone over the phone. "Try one."

"Alright, suit yourself," I say, grimacing already.

This won't take long.

I know just the dress to disabuse Josie of any nostalgic delusions that any of these 'retro' dresses would be suitable for anything other than a laugh.

After wrestling with the taffeta of a hot pink poof-sleeved one in the back of my closet and practically falling over when I finally do get it out, I throw it on and return to the call without so much as a look in the mirror.

The way I figure, if this doesn't convince Josie that my aunt's 'retro steals' are really just her 'things I can't be bothered to throw out so here you go', then nothing will.

Once I point the camera toward me and do a head-to-toe scan, there's a long few moments of utter silence. Then, Josie bursts out laughing.

"Oh, goddamn," she cackles when she finally has enough breath to speak.

"Told you," I say drily. "Now am I allowed to try on the ones I wanted to in the first place? I have less than twenty minutes now to decide."

Still cracking up, she says, "Fine."

The next dress, she goes all quiet.

"I know," I say. "It's not really me. Too low in the front and—"

"Shut up," she says.

"Wow, thanks."

"No, I mean"—already Josie is bobbing her head with determination—"just look. That's it. That's the dress."

Now it's my turn to grumble "fine," although I do head over to my full-length mirror to take a look for myself.

"Am I right, or am I right?" Josie asks.

When I don't answer, she sighs. "OK, OK, I'll shut up."

Which is a good thing, since I'm still not sure what to say.

The woman in the mirror—my reflection—the only thing she has in common with me is a startled expression. She looks... different. Sexy.

Not that I've felt like a complete hag the past year or so, but I haven't felt this... unstoppable for a long while now.

I let my fingertips wander over the teal, slightly metallic panels that make up the dress.

How long have I had this thing stashed in the back of my closet…
and I just put off wearing it, saving it for another night out, another
date?

My reflection nods with determination at me.

Well. Looks like I've found my date.

"You're right," I say. "This is it."

A glance at the time on my phone makes me swear. "Shit! I have
less than ten minutes to pack my bag and get ready the rest of the
way."

"You're welcome," Josie sing-songs. "Have fun! Oh, and Sie?"

"Thanks," I say. "Really."

"Not that," she says with a frown. "Just—you be careful, OK? I'm
sure this guy is fine, just some rich maybe-jerk, but it never hurts to
have your guard up."

"Hello Josie, have you seen me around most guys?" I point out.

Josie chuckles ruefully. "OK, OK, so maybe I should be taking my
own advice. Anyway—bye!"

"Bye!" I say.

And then I'm left with my phone in my hand and my heart in my
throat.

You be careful, OK? OK? OK?

I shake off the thought. Right now, what I need to do is get ready
in the already not-enough time that I have.

A quick coat of mascara, throwing everything by the door in my
purse and I'm out and ready to go.

The elevator takes its sweet time in coming, but by the time I'm
hurrying outside, a glance at my phone finds that it's only 7:04. I
smile.

Not bad.

Neither is the car that's waiting at the curb for me. Although, let's be honest: 'not bad' would be the understatement of the century.

Living in NYC, I've seen plenty of Porsches in person—but never one that I was stepping into.

"Too much?" he asks.

It's then that I realize, that except for a shy smile, I've been completely silent and expressionless since I've gotten into his car.

Maybe I've just been distracted by the immediacy of his presence, how every part of him—from the relaxed set of his broad shoulders to the easy smile on his sculpted face—screams command. Or how, with his hair pulled back and hazel eyes crinkled in a genuine smile, he looks just as handsome as I remember—more, even.

"Not enough," I joke. "I'm used to private jets, but I suppose this will have to do."

As he pulls us back onto the road and gets driving, Nolan's smile is sheepish. "Guess I deserved that. Much worse, probably."

I don't know what to say to that, so I just smile a little.

"I really am sorry about before," Nolan says.

Just like that, all of the ease leaves his body. It's replaced by something tense and hard, yet still sexy.

Ugh.

"If I said I was having the world's worst day that night, that wouldn't be overstating it, believe me." He gives his head a small shake. "Anyway, that's still not an excuse to be as rude as I was to you."

"It's fine," I tell him. "As long as that's the end of it."

God. I feel like a teacher lecturing a naughty child. 'As long as that's the end of it', really?!?

But to my surprise, he just grins, throwing his hand to his head in a salute. "Soldier's honor."

I eye him. "You're in the military?"

The image of him sauntering around in combat burns even sexier in me for some reason.

His smile goes lopsided as he purses his lips. "I didn't mean it like that... but yeah. I was."

"Oh." Hello, sexy veteran stud. "What branch?"

"Navy." The car stopped at a red light, he turns to look at me head-on. In the sunlight, those hazel eyes of his look as green as the sea. Keep your cool. "There wasn't that much action, as you can imagine, but it did me a lot of good. Taught me discipline, and I made some lifelong friends there."

"If you liked it so much, then why did you leave?"

As the light changes and he accelerates the car, something in the stiffening of his neck makes me think that he wants to look me in the eye again, but knows he can't.

"It kind of just happened. News of my mom turned up, and then I got a chance for some comedian gigs... Besides, I had never wanted to stay in the military my whole life. I liked it for what it was, when it was: an experience that set the rest of my life up."

'News of my mom' turning up sounds important—and personal. But I'm not sure we're at the point of sharing important personal stuff. So instead, I say, "You're a comedian now?"

"On and off," he says. "I also help out with the family business from time to time. Right now, I'm overseeing the renovations."

At his scowl, I say, "That bad?"

He chuckles darkly, powerful hands tightening on the steering wheel so that the veins in his tattooed arms stand out. "You'd be surprised how many things our contractor found to fuck up. Goes to show that a friend of a friend isn't a good reason to hire somebody. Anyway, we're ironing out the kinks now, so the next few weeks should be smoother sailing."

As he pulls the Porsche into a parking lot, he continues, "The comedy part of the club being out of business this long, though, the worry is that people will forget about us. People are creatures of habit. Break that and a lot of regulars might not even think to look us up after a while. I can't have that."

Huh. Sexy, manly and intelligent? Sign me the hell up!

"You should do press releases now and leading up to your reopening," I tell him. "Have a few articles commissioned, stuff like that." I smile a little self-consciously. "And I'm not telling you that because I'm a journalist."

Having pulled into a parking spot and turned off the car, Nolan turns to give me that intense gaze head-on. This time it's thoughtful.

"That's an idea," he says.

A smirk pulls his lips to one side. "But first—dinner."

I smile. "Dinner."

Outside, he hurries over to open my door for me.

"What?" he says, at my surprised look. "I can't be a gentleman?"

"Are you?" I say as I step out of the car, the words coming out more questioning than I intended. "A gentleman, I mean?"

The movement brings me breath-close to him, although I quickly step to the side.

Whoa there, Sie, the date just started.

But already, my body feels buzzy and light.

"Alright," Nolan admits, striding beside me as we head to the restaurant. "Got me. I'm no gentleman." His smile is downright irresistible. "Still want to go on this date?"

"Depends," I say, keeping pace, careful not to look over. Despite the way my heart is raging, I know better than to let Nolan set the entire pace for tonight. I hardly know the man. "What do you mean by that?"

Nolan pauses, clearly a bit startled that I would call him out on that. I'm a bit surprised myself.

"Just that..." His easy smile drops. "We have to take what I said seriously?"

I reach for the door handle and open it. Red flag one, though I can't exactly say why. Then again, our texting began with an inadvertent sext, so what did I expect?

"No, of course not," I tell his still uncertain expression. "Of course not."

Inside, though, I'm brought to a stop at what I find.

What. The. Hell.

CHAPTER 7

Nolan

I knew it would impress her. Willow never fails to.

"It's not just the name," Sierra says softly, admiring the tree that fills the four-story building.

I take a few seconds to admire her tousled shoulder-length mahogany hair and wide blue eyes, before shaking my head. "You're looking at the reason this place even exists. Apparently, when the land got passed from a landowner to a developer, the developer was so in love with the tree that he wanted a business that could incorporate it. Thus, Willow was born."

If her expression and gaping red lips are any indication, she's still mesmerized by the 20-foot-tall monolith of a tree.

"What is it?" I ask her as she chuckles.

"It's silly," she says with a dismissive shake of her head.

"I like silly," I tell her. "Tell me."

Another chuckle as she shakes her head, although she answers: "I was just thinking that it reminds me of Grandmother Willow from Pocahontas."

"The greatest willow that ever were," I intone, and we both crack up at that.

Seconds later, the maître d' takes us to our table. Meanwhile, my thoughts return to our car ride.

Sierra Hill.

Goddamn is she something. The sway of those hips, the smile on her lips when I say something funny.

I could do with more of that—a lot more.

Sweet with just the right amount of sass. Lips I'd like to taste.

"Wow," she's saying now. "How did you land this spot, anyway?" She takes a look around, admiring the view from the table we've just been seated at, the only one on the top floor, overlooking the willow and the rest of the restaurant as well.

"Threatened the life of the owner's firstborn child if he didn't comply," I joke.

Her chuckle at my joke buzzes through me. Every smile on those lips is another beckon closer... and closer...

"Honestly?" I say. "The owner was friends with my dad, so I called in a favor."

She nods, sipping at the one of the waters that were here when we arrived.

Putting it down, she says, "So, he was..."

"Colin Storm, yeah."

I spread my arms so they're on the back of my seat. Under the table, her feet don't seem to be in footsie distance.

"I'm sorry for your loss," she says, eyeing me with a bit of confusion.

It takes me a few seconds to realize that I probably don't look like a guy who lost his father recently.

"Thanks. It hit hard at first, but he lived a full life. Was a pretty happy guy. He made all of us around him happy, too."

Before she can say anything, I add: "And not just because he was ridiculously rich, mind you."

She throws up both hands. "I didn't dream of it. There's more to life than money, for sure. Though money does tend to make life easier."

"In some ways," I agree. "In others, not so much. I lost track of the number of women who claimed he fathered children with them and tried to demand staggering amounts of child support—I think it was six or seven over the years. All turned out to be bogus, though apparently my dad had found other ways to piss these women off enough to have them lie to try taking him down." I wave a hand. "Not to play poor little rich boy." I pick up my own water and down the rest in one gulp. "Facts are facts. While Dad and I didn't always see eye-to-eye, especially when I was a teen, he was a good dad."

I frown.

All this reminded me of the shitshow that's in Dad's will.

"Anyway, enough about me," I tell her. "What about you, what are your parents like?"

"My mom's the only one in the picture," she says. "We don't see eye to eye on everything either, but yeah, she's a killer mom."

"Mad respect for single moms," I say, actually meaning it. "Hardest thing on earth to do."

"Agreed," Sierra says. "Although... isn't it just as hard for single dads? I mean the ones who have to go it alone, at least."

"Maybe." I shrug. "Just—the way I see it, usually when something goes to shit in the kid, the first one you blame is the mom. So there's more responsibility on her shoulders, in a way."

At least that's what my mom said, the week before she disappeared. Unless that was just more bullshit...

"I hear you on that," Sierra says with a chuckled nod. "When my older sister used to steal other kids' Lunchables, their moms would call up mine screaming about her being a trash parent and stuff like that. Even though in actuality, Mom was trying everything she could to set Peyton straight: time-outs, punishments, positive reinforcement..."

"What ended up working?" I ask.

"Nothing." Sierra chuckles. "She's still a pretty shitty person, but I'm a bit biased." She frowns. "What about you?"

I smile wide. "How did I end up the stellar success that I am?"

She giggles, shaking her head. "No—siblings?"

"A bunch," I say. "Greyson's the oldest. Then there's Landon and me, we're twins. Emerson is the youngest."

"A twin. That must've been..." She trails off, clearly unsure what 'that must've been'.

"Fun? Yes." A smile quirks on one side of my face. "Annoying? Also yes."

"I was known as the fuck-up, awkward twin," I add with a cutesy smile. "In case you were wondering. At least in high school, that is."

She manages a slight smile as she shakes her head. "I can't see you being awkward."

"I had a stutter." I frown. Sometimes, even just thinking about it brings me back. Tonight's chock-full of things pulling me back to the past, the last place I want to go. "It really messed with my head, had me smoking, hanging out with a pretty rough crowd. Cue: Dad having the bright idea to send me into the military. Well, I say bright idea, but it actually was a bright idea. Even helped me get rid of my stutter."

Since when am I sharing my whole life story with this girl?

"Enough about me," I say, and as she chuckles, I throw up both hands. "OK, OK, I mean it this time."

As the waitress approaches, I order us a fine red wine, then get back to our conversation. "What about you? What were you like in high school?" I look her up and down with a knowing smirk. "The same?"

"Because you know me so well?" she sasses me with a little smirk of her own. "Yeah, I guess I wasn't overly different, just a bit more scared I guess. Of letting down my mom—failing out of school or ending up a teenage pregnancy case like she was—which is the last thing she wanted for me."

"You're not scared now?" I ask.

Despite my jokey tone, her blue gaze cuts to mine. When she speaks, there's no joke in it. "A little bit. You?"

I meet those blue eyes, the kind you could drown in and not even realize you've hit water. "We're all scared."

A few seconds, that pass too fast. So fast, that only after them do I realize I missed my cue to kiss her.

A minute or so later, the waiter shows up with our wine.

"On a happier note." I lift my glass once he's gone, eyes on her. "Here's to wine."

"To wine," Sierra says, lifting her glass.

We order our meals and they're delivered not long after: two delicious plates of roasted lamb, followed by chocolate cheesecake.

Then, after dessert, more wine, and then, it's time to kiss her.

Really, it was time to kiss her the moment I laid eyes on her. Or the second we sat down here. Or after my 'scared' comment and that missed moment.

Still, there's now. Better late than never.

"Hey," I say softly, leaning in.

"Hey," she says quietly.

Her eyes flit with a cocktail of fear and excitement as I lean in further to cover her mouth with mine.

CHAPTER 8

Sierra

Just as his lips are about to land on mine, he says, "Want a job?"

I freeze, staring at him blankly, as he moves back to sit in his seat like nothing happened.

Am I going crazy, or were we this close to having a moment? And did he just offer me…

"A job?" I say blankly.

"Sorry, I shouldn't have assumed…" Nolan trails off, that boyish smile still endearing even under the circumstances. "Are you free? To work, I mean—would you have time to take on another project?"

"This is kind of sudden." I eye him, waiting for the 'kidding!' or giveaway chuckle that doesn't come.

"Yeah, well, I'm a sudden kind of guy." Again, that smile, which I now find slightly less endearing—he's actually being serious? "Will you do it?"

"Do what? All you asked me was if I wanted a job."

"True." He bobs his head a few times, mulling it over. Who hires people on a whim? Nolan Storm, I guess. "Alright, here's what I think. We could use some of those press articles you were telling me about. It's a damn good idea. Keep the comedy club in the news until we're back in business. What do you think? Are you interested?"

"I… Maybe?"

Is this actually happening? Did the hottest guy I've been on a date with in, well, ever just almost kiss me and hire me instead?

"Yeah, sorry." He has the decency to look a bit chagrined, although it doesn't dim his obvious excitement. "It is a lot at once. No rush."

I rise. Whatever happened or is happening here tonight, I'm not going to figure it out by sitting here and trying not to drool over how extra-handsome Nolan looks when he's excited and chagrined at the same time.

"You have to go?" he asks, disappointed.

"Yeah, I... need to think about all this."

You just got cockblocked by a job opportunity is what happened, sister. WTF.

"Right." He rises too. "I'll drive you home."

On the way back, we don't talk. After all the talking we did, I don't mind some silence now. Gives me some space to begin to collect myself.

Besides, maybe he's waiting for the more stereotypical time to have a goodnight kiss—at the end of the date?

But when he pulls up to my apartment building, his look is once again one of chagrin, not lust.

"Sorry if I put you on the spot back there. No pressure."

"Thanks, I..." I open the car door. My cheeks feel hot, and I feel like running away, laughing nervously and sighing all at the same time. "I'll definitely think about it. Night."

"Night," he says, starting to say something else, but me shutting the door cuts it off.

I pause, looking at him questioningly. He just laughs and waves me on.

Back at my place, I don't waste any time calling up the twins.

"Holy moly," Josie says when I tell them about our almost-kiss replaced by an actual job offer.

"What state are your lips in?" Wynona wonders instead. "Did you forget lip chap again?"

"That's it," I say drily. "The horrendously cracked state of my lips drove him off—so peeling they were like a blistered sunburn, his eyes were burned by the hideousness that was my lips."

"And this is why you're a journalist," Josie says, and I can almost hear her nod. "A way with words. Though Wynona—you bitch!"

"What—it's a possibility," Wynona protests.

"And so is you getting leprosy and your limbs falling off, but you don't see me just mentioning that to you!" Josie snaps back.

"It's OK," I say, before this breaks out into all-out war. I've been with the twins many many times when they fight, and it's definitely not pretty. "Although it is really weird."

"Think he chickened out?" Josie says, making a bawk-bawk noise that sends us all cracking up.

"You saw the man," I reply, deadpan, once I'm done laughing. "Why would he, of all people, chicken out? He probably has girls like me for breakfast."

"Correction," Josie cuts in. "He has girls like you never because you are a one-of-a-kind, darling."

"Thanks, J," I say.

"Are you going to take the job?" Wynona demands. "You'd be a fool not to."

"Wynona!" Josie snaps.

"Yeah, yeah," she mutters.

"Wyn's probably right, though," I admit. "Even if it'll be kind of weird working for a guy I went on a date with, at least it's a job? And not the Pancake House?"

"That's it," Josie says soothingly. "Focus on the positive."

"On that note," I say. "Horatio hasn't pooped on my new rug yet."

"Wow, luck is just flying your way left, right and center," Josie says cheerily. "Now, call him."

Said in the same chirpy tone, the second part of her words throw me for a loop. "Huh? Now?"

"Why not?" she insists.

"Because it's… I don't know… ten o'clock at night and I'm about to go to bed?"

"She's right," Wynona says heavily. "What if he meets another hot journalist in the next hour? Better jump on that job op quick."

"This is a great opportunity," Josie continues soothingly. "You said it yourself. Nolan probably has some great connections too, maybe even to get you more work if you do well. So call him—do it."

"Do it," Wynona insists. "Don't be a pussy."

"Do it," Josie insists. Then, in a scolding tone, "Don't be mean, Winnie."

At her hated nickname from when we were kids, Wynona sighs.

"OK, OK," I say, more to shut them up than anything. "I'll do it. Bye?"

"You better," the twins chorus, then chuckle. "Night, Sie."

Seconds later, before I can talk myself out of it or come up with any of the very good reasons why this is a bad idea, I call Nolan up.

"Wow, that was fast," he says, picking up right away. "Not that I'm complaining."

"I didn't say that I'd take the job," I point out.

"So you already decided that you don't want the job without even knowing the salary or anything?"

"Those details you can email me. I'll send you my email address tomorrow. But as long as we're not talking minimum wage, I'm in."

"Yeah?" He's grinning; I'd put money on it. Hell, I'm grinning too.

"Yeah!" I say. "I actually like your comedy club, so it'll be a fun story to do."

"Oh, hey, I'm not talking story—there's going to be stories! Lots of them." He chuckles. "Sorry, I probably sound like an overexcited tool. Hey, but I am right now. You know what? Tomorrow morning, let's do this, get started. The renos are delayed enough as it is, let's not delay this. If you're free?"

"Yeah, I..." Holy shit, tomorrow. "Sure. Nine AM works?"

"Nine AM is perfect," he says. "You'll see, Sierra. This is going to be great."

"I'm excited," I say.

After we've hung up, I sit down on my old corduroy couch that sinks in the middle. Horatio comes over and plops on my lap, giving me a disingenuously knowing look.

Because really, I have to wonder: Are Nolan and I excited for the same things?

**

The next morning, I'm up bright and way too early. I give Horatio a walk, he terrorizes some pigeons, then I gulp down some chili ramen. Finally, at 8:30, I put on my best work suit and hurry off.

Nolan's waiting for me in the restaurant part when I arrive. It's closed, and you can hear the sounds of construction from the comedy club part.

"Hey! You look great."

I pause, smiling with embarrassment and stifling my inner frustration.

This man could get a medal for his ability to mess with my head.

"Come in," he says, with that grin that makes me want to grin too. "I've got a surprise for you."

You're here for a job, Sierra. Remember that.

"Look at this," he crows, walking me over to a room that's as far from the renovations as you can be while still being in the same building. "Your own office." He hastily moves some papers. "Of course, if you're still sure that you want the job, obviously. I almost forgot—the salary is $40 an hour, but we're not paying for you to get glasses or some shit like that. No benefits."

"Oh."

Forty dollars an hour? Mic drop.

"That good with you?" he asks.

"That's definitely good with me." I try to keep my smile from looking too insane or shocked, lest he change his mind.

"Well, then." He pauses, looking around, although his gaze keeps stopping on me. Maybe my work outfit is a tad too tight? "I'll let you get to work, then. First article is all you. Just remind our customers that the restaurant is still here, still open and we still love them. I'm going to run to check on the renos, but feel free to check in with anything that you need. Anything at all."

Did I imagine the husky tone for that last part?

Anyway, he's leaving, gone now.

And it's just me, in my office, getting paid $40 to do what I love!

I do a little victory dance for a few seconds, then get to work. I am getting paid for it, after all.

I dash out an article in record time, then brainstorm ideas for a few others while I'm at it.

Then, a knock on my door.

"Come in," I call.

Nolan pokes his head in. "Hey. It's lunchtime. I was just wondering if you wanted to go for..."

He frowns, stepping inside. "OK. Fuck that. What I really came in here for, is to do this."

He strides towards me purposefully and only once his lips land on mine do I realize that he's actually doing this.

We're doing this.

His lips against mine blot out everything else.

The force of them, the command. The slightest hint of tongue, then more.

This is everything.

His hands cup my face, his body presses to mine.

As soon as the first thought breaks free, it spills out in words as I pull away. "But Nolan, now we work together and—"

He kisses the next words out of my lips. "This doesn't have to change anything."

Which is fine as fuck with me since this man kissing me is all I can think about. All I can be with.

The kiss moves me down onto the desk behind me, presses our bodies further together.

All thought edges away. All that's left is his lips guiding mine. His hands stroking me, like they're memorizing my shape.

Nolan Storm. Nolan fucking Storm...

The kiss develops fast and hot and fluid.

Our lips twist as he undoes the top button of my shirt, then the next, and the next.

My hands venture under his shirt to enjoy his muscles. Hello, six-pack heaven...

Meanwhile, he tosses my shirt to the side.

Mid-kiss, I pause. "But Nolan—"

"You're right," he says gruffly, striding to the door and locking it. Then he lowers the blinds. His smile lands on me. "That's better. Now, come here."

I smirk right back at him, although inside I'm a thrash of uncertainty, want and more want. "And if I won't?"

"Easy." He smirks, striding for me, closing the distance between us in two quick paces. "I'll make you."

Next thing I know, he's picked me up and pressed me against the wall. The hard wall behind me, his taut body in front of me, the hardness between his legs pressing out of his work pants into me... holy fuck.

This is really happening.

"Wanted to do this," he says, kissing me, then pulling away to get a good look at me as his hands stroke my breasts over my bra. "For too fucking long now."

And then his hands meet together behind my back, undo my bra and let it fall to the floor.

He growls with approval, cupping one bare breast in one hand, then the other in the other. His eyes close with pleasure as he caresses them. "Fucking perfect."

Our lips meet again. I peel off his shirt—it's only fair—enjoying his newly-bared muscles and the tattoos. All in black, there's quotes in other languages, a clock splitting into storms and mammoths, a shape that looks like a country…

He guides my hands admiring his muscles down. "Not quite as interesting as what's going on down here…"

"Oh yeah?" I say, feeling bold and grabbing him over his pants.

Something warms in me.

Oh hell yes is he hard.

"Yeah," he growls, with one final squeeze of my breasts before he hikes my skirt up.

His caressing hands move closer and closer, while I can't seem to take my hands off his crazy-hard cock.

So massive and perfect and hard…

Meanwhile, he's caressing my thighs so exquisitely that my whole body is atremble.

In one smooth motion, he picks me up and places me on the edge of my desk. Then he takes another good second to take me all in. "That's better."

He gives the desk a pat. "I knew this thing would come in handy."

"Oh yeah?" I say.

Him kissing me again is the answer. His tongue strokes mine while his fingers stroke their way higher and higher.

When he finally presses his fingers into the wetness over my panties, I groan.

"Wet as fuck," he says approvingly.

Right before he slips his fingers under my panties and inside me.

"Oh," I groan, as his fingers flicker in me.

They're just teasing my opening for now, but fuck does it feel amazing.

Then, dipping in a bit further, and a bit further, and... "Fuuuuuuuck," I moan.

Nolan smirks. "There something else you want in there?"

As he finger-fucks my pussy nice and good, another wail falls out of me.

"That's it," he growls.

Next thing I know, his pants and briefs are on the ground and he's edging his cock into me. Just teasing the opening.

It feels fucking amazing.

"Fuck you," I moan.

"You want it?" he says, dipping it in slightly.

"Please," I groan.

"Then have it," he growls, shoving himself into me.

Pleasure explodes through me.

Oh fuck am I having it. All of it. Every inch of his perfect width and length.

My whole body trembles with it. My speech breaks down into monosyllables from it.

This man. This fucking man. What he does to me...

"Fuck yeah," he growls, exhaling raggedly. "You, Sierra Hill..." He trails off, frowning.

My pussy clasps frantically at his cock and he moves in and out of me again. And again. And a-fucking-gain.

In and out. Deep and deeper. More and fucking more.

My climax explodes over me, but Nolan isn't near done.

Turning me around so that I'm face-first on the desk, he fucks me some more. I wail into the unforgiving wood grain of my desk.

Being fucked here… on my desk… by my boss…

…And it feels fucking amazing.

As another climax rips through me and a scream throttles out of me, Nolan slaps a hand over my mouth. "I don't want any interruptions."

And with that, he fucks me harder than ever. Until I can't think anymore, can hardly breathe. Until all I know, all I care about is the pulse of him, the in and out, the more upon more.

Until we're clasped, coming together for the final time.

CHAPTER 9

Nolan

She screws with my head like a broken can-opener.

Her on my lap in my arms feels damn good. Damn right.

Almost as though if we just sat here smiling dopily at each other how we are, maybe fucked a couple more times, that would be the most worthwhile day I've had in a while.

I frown.

Clearly, I need to get up and do some real work.

"Guess what?" I say.

"What?" Sierra says.

"I think we're going to get along just fine," I say, giving her a little pat.

As I get up and start to pull on my briefs, she says, "What does that mean?"

I'm no expert on women, but any idiot could tell that that tone is bad news.

"Did you just hire me... for this?" she asks quietly, gaze drilling into me. "So that we'd..."

"No." I let the khakis in my hand drop to the floor. Then I put on a playful pouty face. "Did you just say yes... for this?"

"Of course." She rolls her eyes although she can't hold back an amused giggle. "I only accept jobs from guys I'm attracted to."

I manage a smile. "Glad I made the cut then."

"Seriously, though," she says, starting to put on her own clothes. "Is this going to make things weird now?"

"Not unless you want them to be."

"Why would I want them to be?"

"I don't know. Why are we still talking about this?"

Buttoning up her blouse, she pauses. For some reason, her face looks guilty. "There's something you should know."

"What—that was even better than you expected?" I joke.

"You're not one for humbleness, are you?" she asks lightly.

I manage to look chagrined, and mean it. "I joke when I get nervous. Sue me."

"You're nervous?"

"Are you just going to leave me hanging here?" I say, to deflect her from what I just said.

"It's about when we first met. Your phone." She says the words in a flat voice, like stating the ingredients of tomato soup. "I went through it."

Lounging on the wall, I stand up stick-straight. "What?"

"My friends hacked into it first—your finger code thing was easy, then we looked through some of your pictures."

"That's it?" I ask, my own voice flat and cool now.

Now she's glaring at me, like I'm the one who went through her phone. "Oh yeah, we also stayed half a year in the tropics and charged it on the Visa card saved on your phone, almost forgot." Smoothing her ruffled red-brown hair down, she gives her head a little shake. "Yeah, that's it."

"Oh, right." I make for the door. "Good to know. Well, this was…" I open the door and walk out of it. "I'll be seeing you."

It's only once I'm back in the restaurant part of the building that I scowl.

Maybe rushing out of there wasn't the best thing to do, but I have no clue where my head is at.

All I know is, what she told me threw me for a loop. And not a good one.

Later in the day, I text her some more tips for the article she's doing for us. I'm careful to stay away from her actual office.

I still have no idea where my head is at, or if I even want to know.

I'm just getting in my car to head home from work when Emerson calls me up. "You busy tonight?"

"Nope." Something that I instinctively know I want to avoid flickers in me—and I dismiss it. "Why?"

"I... she dumped me, Nolan."

"Maude?"

"No. Mary." He sighs. "It doesn't matter, though. She dumped me this afternoon. Wouldn't even tell me why."

"Shit, that bitch."

"She's not a bitch." Another sigh. "OK, she's no star either. I don't know."

"You want to go out tonight?" he continues.

"Do I ever." Suddenly, all the swirling in my head materializes into one certain fact: I need a nice wild night out. "Jax might be up for it too. He and Laura have been on the fritz lately. If we're lucky and use some good old brotherly guilt tripping, maybe we can even get Landon to show."

"No need." The sound of a piano note trills through the line—Emerson probably called me up during one of his piano seshes. He actually does a bunch of piano scales to help him relax, imagine!

"Don't pressure him into it or anything. I just thought for tonight, if you were down—"

"Stop it," I growl at him. "Tonight is happening."

"OK," he says, clearly relieved. "Just text me where you wanna go for whenever. And I'll see you then?"

"Yeah." I say. "See you then."

Another experimental note sounds from his end, and his voice sounds happier when he reaffirms, "See you then."

I fritter away the next few hours with some heated-up leftover falafels. Jax swings by too, his face grim.

"That bad?" I ask.

He shrugs. "She threw a microwave at me. Last year, I was all for her getting into CrossFit, thought she could work off her anger problems, but now…"

I sigh in commiseration, go over to give him a supportive brotherly pat. "Now this cold-blooded psycho has even more tools at her violent disposal."

He shrugs my hand away. "Fuck off."

"You know I'm just honest with you because I love you," I sing-song after him as he stalks to the fridge. "And yeah, please, just help yourself. I have some moldy apples in there that need some love."

His back to me as he scans the (admittedly dismal) fridge contents, he gives me the finger. I blow him a kiss, even though he can't see it.

"Here," I say, and slide him a plate with the sixth falafel that I wasn't sure I even wanted anyway. "And do I ever have the plan tonight for you."

He swings around to take the falafel, although the look on his freckled face is suspicious.

"What?" I ask innocently.

"Last time you had that tone, we almost got arrested for filling the Gramercy Park fountain with bubbles and dancing in it with those two crazy sisters from Japan."

"And?" I eye him. "That was still the best night ever! Plus, key word, almost."

When he doesn't respond, I continue, "Anyway, tonight's fun will likely be of the tamer variety. We're just going out to cheer up Emerson who's been recently... ahem, released into the wild."

Jax whistles low in understanding. "Poor guy. Magda left him?"

"I think it was Maggie," I comment.

"Nah, was definitely Magda," he states.

"Well." I smile pleasantly. "Just another reason for you to come, so we can find out this mystery bitch's name."

The smile on his face is part grim and part excited. "OK. I'm in."

I try calling up Landon, but he doesn't pick up. Probably doing some batty family thing like a sock puppet show or baking pink chocolate cookies or something.

So I leave a voicemail: "Hey, this is your twin brother. Remember him? We're going out tonight and you should come, Emerson needs your big brotherly presence. If you need an alibi, I can tell the old wifey that we're volunteering at a homeless shelter for leprous children who are also blind, deaf, and mute, if that would help. Bye."

Not that I actually expect him to show. Ever since he got ensnared by said wifey, Landon has been MIA.

The next few hours, Jax and I shoot the shit, watch some of the basketball game, order some shawarma. Then, finally, it's time to head to Svitz.

"Emerson's going to meet us there," I tell Jax in the cab. "He's too cheap to take the $25 taxi ride over to our place ahead of time."

I spare my little brother the embarrassment of revealing to Jax that really, he just blew thousands on this Maggie who summarily dumped him.

We find Emerson at the bar, a sad-looking slob with one empty tequila and two finished ones already.

His blond hair is askew, and his blue eyes are rimmed with red. Poor guy.

I give him a big slapping hug. "Don't you worry. Tonight is going to be epic."

He tries to smile, but all it does is turn his grimace into a somewhat neutral expression. "She dumped me."

I nod, trying to look more sympathetic than I'm feeling. If he had asked me, the woman was a right nutto. But no one asked me, so…

"Got that much. But look!" I inject some surprised enthusiasm in my voice as I gesture around us. "This place is full of hot women who aren't bitches!"

Emerson makes a noncommittal sound, not that I blame him. Just a quick glance around this packed place found at least 20 gorgeous women… and zero interest from me.

I scowl.

Normally, by now, I'd already have scoped out my first choice for the night… and the second …and the third.

Who knows what the fuck is up with me.

Just then, Jax comes back from the bar. He gives Emerson a sympathetic nod. "I heard what happened—sorry about that."

"See?" I tell my baby brother. "Jax here also has terrible taste in women. You two have so much in common!"

Two angry glares go at me.

"It's not like your own taste in women is anything other than questionable," Jax points out, running his hand through his red hair as he keeps on glaring at me. "Didn't that one chick try to rob you?"

"She did rob me," I inform him indignantly. "My best Rolex, too."

He shrugs, his point proven.

"Anyway." I try to smile with pleasant patience at the two buzzkills. "That's not why we're here. We're here to forgot our troubles, whatever or whoever they may be. So—first shot's on me!"

The second one ends up being on me too, and the third. By the fourth, I've pulled them onto the dance floor, while some good future house mix has everyone grooving, and gotten Emerson a distraction for tonight. She's short, with gorgeous copper skin, slightly buggy eyes, and curvy as hell.

She's even got a lookalike friend who's laughing way too hard at all my jokes that I would normally be all over, except for tonight.

For whatever reason.

Then, just as Jax finds his own willowy blonde to cheer him up, mine starts grinding on me, and I make some unlikely excuse and leave. Not for good, just to get some air.

Outside, I lounge at the curb and glare at the dark flower shop storefront across the street.

What the fuck is up with me tonight?

"Nolan," a familiar voice says.

"You actually came," I say, seeing who it is.

"I actually came," Landon repeats, looking as surprised about it as I am, with his hands shoved into his leather jacket coat pockets. "How's Emerson doing?" he asks, glancing at the club.

Another future house song with a great beat echoes out to us.

"Great, actually," I tell Landon. "You should see this girl he's pulled. Gorgeous."

Landon nods. "Guess that's something. Normally, I'd say give it time, but it seems this Malinda really did a number on his head."

"You mean Maggie," I tell him.

"Nah, she was definitely named Malinda," he says. "Although you can't be blamed for not remembering her name, since the woman refused to meet any of us. That should've been warning sign #1.

"And you?" he adds before I can respond.

I eye him. "What do you mean, and me?"

He raises his eyebrows with a shrug. "Normally you'd be right in there with them, with your own girl or two for the night. Instead you're out here, looking glum. Why?"

I shrug. "Guess my twindar kicked in and I sensed your nearness, so I came out here to meet with you."

He snorts. "Really, now."

"Really now." I throw a hand to my chest and continue on in a woo-woo voice. "When will you accept that our connection is celestial, eternal..."

Landon just shakes his head. "Cut the shit."

I glare at him. "Fine, have it your way."

We stand there, out in the cool, out with the smokers, and some far-off wino calling to someone who's not there. The smoke still has a bit of a beckon to me—I used to be a pack-a-day-er way back when, although it's been a long time since I kicked the habit.

Some things you never get over completely, though.

"So," he says.

"It's just an off night," I say. "Happens to the best of us."

"Oh yeah?"

I throw him a derisive look. "You here to be my psych or my brother? We're supposed to be here for Emerson, anyway."

He shrugs. "Sounds like he doesn't need us. Anyway, I'm just telling it how I see it."

"And how I see it is…" I trail off. Who the fuck am I kidding? There's no harm in saying it, anyway. "It's just this girl I met. It's not going to go anywhere, but I just thought… she seemed really cool. And then I found out I couldn't trust her."

He swings a sidelong assessing gaze my way. "You got robbed again?"

"No!" I sputter indignantly. "Why does everyone always remember that?"

"Because the way you told it was funny?" Landon says with a shrug. "Crazy skinny little emo white girl ends up beating you up when you're smashed and stealing your Rolex after you fucked."

"Don't remind me," I say drily. "Though no, nothing on that scale, thankfully."

Landon doesn't say anything. But now that it's out, I might as well get the rest of that shit out, too. "She went through my phone."

"Oh." He pauses, as if waiting for something more. When I say nothing, he adds, "Is that it?"

"Is that it?" I glare at him. "Oh, I'm sorry—is that not an invasion of privacy for dads who have much more important things to worry about?"

"Nah, it still is pretty shitty," he admits with a half shrug. "I just thought when you said that you couldn't trust her, we were talking about some major betrayal. Like her banging your cousin. Or stealing your Rolex."

I keep on glaring at him.

"Was it when you were sleeping?" Landon asks.

"No, it was before we even went on a date, after I'd been kind of a jerk to her and dropped my phone accidentally into her..." Realizing that I'm pacing, I force myself to stop. "What the hell does it matter? It's still a sketchy thing to do. Even if it was her friends who hacked into it—she looked at my photos, man!"

"You still have those funny Arctic glamour nudes?" Landon asks with a chuckle.

"No, that's not the point!" I open my mouth, then close it.

I sound like a butthurt idiot. So what if she went through my phone? It wasn't even her idea.

"You sure that's the reason you're upset?" Landon asks. He shrugs again. "Then again, I'm not your psych, just your twin. Anyway. Are we going to spend the night out here arguing, or go in and make sure Emerson's night ends well too?"

My answer is to stride back into the club. Coming out here was the problem in the first place. I don't need more time to think. Fuck it, I don't need any time to think at all. That was the problem in the first place.

Inside, Emerson's still with his girl, their arms around each other, and Jax with his, moving along to the slower beat of the music. Mine is long gone, and who the hell knows why I feel relieved.

The rest of the night is more fun—we get on the dance floor and dance until we're exhausted. We go out for burgers after, then go our separate ways.

Jax and his girl take the spare bedroom. I go into mine and sit on the bed.

Now that I can't put it off any longer—what I didn't even realize I was putting off until now—I pick up the phone.

CHAPTER 10

Sierra

What could it have been about?

I eye my phone suspiciously, but Nolan left no message when he called me up at four AM after an entire day of avoiding me after I told him about the phone thing.

I put my phone away with a final frown.

No way am I going to be some afterthought booty call, if that's what he had in mind. If not, well… then he could have left a voicemail. Or even just a text.

Now, it's eight AM, and still no word from him. Whatever.

For breakfast, I have some ramen with paprika. Then I walk Horatio, who only chases one other dog, probably since most have the good sense to stay away after he barks at them a few times.

Then, at home, I cave.

"You what?!?" Josie exclaims as soon as I tell her over the phone.

"Knew it," Wynona says in a tone that could be good or bad or anything in between.

"Yeah, well," I say, finding I can't say anything else.

"So, it was amazing then?" Josie presses.

"Do you have to even ask?" I say with a sigh. "Yes, the sex was crazy amazing."

"And…" Josie's tone goes hesitant. "How do you feel about it?"

"Honestly?" I collapse-sit onto the couch and gesture Horatio over from the floor. He sits there and blinks at me. Sometimes I think he's more cat than dog. "I'm not really sure. Afterwards, we kind of cuddled for a bit, but then I blurted out something stupid and it ruined everything."

"Did you tell him about that time we made a voodoo doll of your bully and stuck pins in it?" Wynona asks.

"No—what? Why would I even…"

"Ignore her," Josie mutters. "She's trying this weird new nootropic and it's been making her blurt out the randomest shit these past few days."

"It isn't random asking the cashier all the different countries all the unlabeled apples come from," Wynona argues. "It's not."

"Can I say what I was going to?" I cut in.

"Of course," Josie says. "What happened?"

"I admitted that we looked in his phone and he went all quiet and left."

Silence.

"Huh," Josie says.

"Tool," Wynona says heatedly. "Like that's worse than the worst thing he's ever done."

"I don't even know what I was thinking in the first place, telling him like that, or even sleeping together at work in the first place," I say sadly. "That's the thing—I wasn't thinking. It all just happened so fast…" I sink deeper into the couch, part of me wishing it could just envelop me completely. "Jesus, guys, I had sex with my boss on my first day on the job."

"Well," Wynona says. "When you put it like that…"

"Ignore her," Josie cuts in. "It's his own damn fault for offering you a job when he was about to kiss you instead."

"I don't know for sure that he was about to kiss me," I point out. "I could've misread the situation."

She snorts. "Yeah, because I've always been offered jobs when the person is leaning across the table going for my lips. Especially judging by what happened once you were alone in the office, yeah, I'd say he was about to kiss you."

"You're probably right," I say. "Still. It feels shitty. What if I just screwed up the best job opportunity I've had in years?"

"It's better than holding a dark secret inside," Wynona murmurs. "It'll eat you from the inside out, until you're a shell of what you could've been."

"Thanks, Eeyore," Josie grumbles to her sister. "Although she has a point. It's better that the truth about his phone is out there. If the man freaks over it, then that's his problem. Anyway—you want to come over? I got this new cranberry pancake mix and even Wyn is crazy about it, and—"

"Wish I could," I say. "But I told my mom I'd stop by this afternoon. She's been pretty down since her latest break-up."

"Oh, no worries." Josie's tone is sympathetic. "Joe was no good?"

"Nah, it was Lew, but yeah."

"What is with your mother and men with three-letter names?" Wynona asks. "Joe, Dan, Lew, Jay, Cal."

"Holy shit," I say, realizing she's right.

We all crack up at that.

"Maybe that's her type?" I say. "Anyway, I really do have to go. Love you."

After I hang up and head out for Mom's, it occurs to me that I never told my friends the most pressing thing of all: I think I might actually like this guy.

Mom comes to the door with a half-finished hat she was knitting in hand, although that isn't fooling anyone. I can see that her makeup is smudged, her smile tremulous.

I give her a big hug.

"How's my working girl?" she asks.

"Good," I say. "Still riding on Cloud 9 a bit that I even got this job at all."

As we walk into the TV room to sit down, Mom turns off Dirty Dancing. I don't mention how we both know that's her breakup cry movie.

"It is good," she continues hesitantly. "But after that contract is done, maybe it would be worth looking into..."

"Mom," I cut her off. "Please."

"Fine, fine." Another smile.

"Enough about me," I say. "How are you doing?"

"Oh, you know me." A brave smile that doesn't touch her eyes. "I'm... well, keeping on."

"Screw Lew," I tell her. "He was an idiot."

This smile is only in her eyes; her mouth goes pained. "Maybe. But I was the one who chose him, honey."

I lean over to give her another hug. "Everyone makes mistakes."

She shakes her head, sinking onto the couch as she murmurs out the next words, half to herself: "I should know better by now. Men can't be trusted. Your father certainly couldn't be. They leave as soon as the going gets tough."

Seeing my face, she quickly adds, "Sorry. I shouldn't have brought your father up."

"It's fine," I tell her.

Mainly because I don't want to admit that this time I wasn't thinking about my dad at all. I was thinking about Nolan, his face ice-cold as he strode out of the room.

And that call last night…

"Anyway, I don't want you to make the same mistakes as me. I go from trusting men too much to not enough." A low, bitter laugh. "You go make your own mistakes, honey. God knows you have a better head on your shoulders than I did at your age."

"Stop, Mom," I say, instead of what I really want to.

Part of me wants to blurt out what happened with Nolan, get it out: that I don't have such a good head on my shoulders after all. That I might've majorly screwed up.

For some reason, Mom trusts implicitly that I know what I'm doing when it comes to men, but not at all when it comes to my career.

But I don't want to dash her view of me, especially when she's dealing with her own hurt. Yes, Mom has enough to handle right now—better not to upset her.

"Anyway," she says, rising. "Enough moping. Want to help me make a nice bowl?"

I smile. This is half the reason I come. Not to cheer Mom up—I'm not so good at that—but to help her cheer herself up.

That's the thing about Mom, she'll mope like crazy when she's alone—for days, weeks, even months, if left to her own devices—but as soon as there's another person in the room, she'll straighten herself up, put on a not-quite-genuine smile that still does the job, and get busy.

A few minutes later, as the wheel rolls and the bowl begins to form from the clay I'm shaping with my fingers, with Mom smiling softly to herself, she shoots a smile my way. "Thanks for this, Sierra."

I want to thank her too. Pottery is her passion, but it's hard to think of other things while the bowl is being shaped between your fingers.

And today, I need all the distraction I can get.

We've moved on to the next bowl, with Mom working on it herself, when a familiar knock-knock-kna-knock-knock hits the door.

I freeze as Mom stops the wheel, wipes off her hands, and quickly goes to the door.

"Oh," she says from the hallway. "Look who it is."

"Did I come at a bad time?" Peyton's voice rings so loud that it comes into the room as if she were here instead of at the door.

I find my fingers instinctively clenching on the end of the tabletop.

Next second, she's sashaying into the room, bedecked in Louis Vuitton plastered with in-your-face monograms. Her potent perfume hits me first. It smells like cupcakes, if several generations of stinky, sugary cupcakes had babies together to produce the stinkiest, sugariest cupcake of all.

"Oh, Sierra. I didn't realize you were here." She gives me a smile. "I'm sure you've been helping Mom—but can you believe I got her a complete spa package at Nordica?"

"Oh, I can," I say flatly.

"I heard about your new job," she continues. "And that means you've met Nolan Storm? Well, you have to ask him if he knows Tom Cruise—I bumped into him at our company party the other day."

And so, the contest begins again...

I can't get to the door fast enough.

"Honey?" Mom asks. "Where are you going?"

"I'm sorry," I say, mind racing for an excuse—any decent, leave-worthy excuse. "I just remembered... I have something... something... very unmissable and very... Bye?"

I'm out the door before I can see the disappointment on Mom's face. Mom never gives up hoping that Peyton and I will magically become BFFs, the poor woman.

As I'm heading for my car, my phone rings with another call... from Nolan. I reject it.

Right now, I'm not in a good headspace to deal with whatever he's calling me about. Even if it's good.

I've never claimed Mom is a good role model for her relationships with men, but still. Part of me sometimes wonders if she's right. Can men be trusted?

Anyway, getting involved with Nolan Storm when he's my boss seems like just asking for trouble.

And not the good kind.

I spend the rest of the day getting some errands done. I buy some groceries for my woefully empty pantry. I even splurge and pick up some dark chocolate wine for the twins and I next time we hang.

They both have dates tonight, so I crack into some of it myself.

I even give Horatio a bit of bacon, which results in some thankful face-licking.

I clean my room, go through my closet and finally, when there's nothing else I can do to put it off, I call up Nolan.

"Hey," he says.

"Hey," I say. "I just wanted to say that I understand your position."

Wait now, where the hell is this coming from?

"My position?" he asks.

"About us. That it's probably not a good idea for us to get involved."

The more I'm saying, the more it feels like a weight is being lifted off me.

"I said that?" Nolan sputters.

"You don't have to," I say coolly. "Anyway, see you on Monday."

And then I hang up.

"There," I tell Horatio, who's eyeing me like I have some more bacon and am simply hiding it. "It's as simple as that."

Although it doesn't feel that simple at all.

Especially not when I reject Nolan's next call.

First, I'll give him time to think about what I said, not just call me up and argue with me as a knee-jerk reaction. Maybe he'll come to see that I'm doing both of us a favor.

Sunday, the twins and I go for a hike—Josie's idea—which Wynona moans about, at least until we ditch her at the trailhead and come back to find her with a tatted-up ranger who is describing different types of flora and fauna, which, more surprisingly, she actually seems interested in.

Anyway, Monday comes quickly enough. One minute, I'm gulping down ramen in the car at the stoplight while driving there, determined not to be late; the next, I'm hurrying into the office, scrubbing the last of the ramen out of my teeth with my tongue.

Going in the side entrance, I manage to avoid him, and I'm just at my office when: "Hey."

I freeze. So much for avoiding him.

"Hey," I say. "Good weekend?"

Now isn't the best time to notice how painfully handsome he looks in that plain white tee, the one that shows off his black-tatted arms, the arms that held me, stroked me… and…

A tremor goes through me.

Oh, fuck it all.

"Not really," he says. "You?"

"It was alright. Got to go for a hike, which was nice. Anyway, I'm almost done with that second article. I'll probably be sending it your way for approval this afternoon. As for the third—"

"Sierra," he blurts out. "I wanted to apologize. For overreacting how I did when you told me about going through my phone."

"Hey, it's not a big deal," I say, forcing my voice steady. If only I could force my heart steady too. "What happened between us before that, us getting… involved, probably wasn't a good idea anyway."

He stands there for a few seconds, digesting my words.

"If you say so," he says finally. Then he leaves.

My shoulders, which I hadn't even realized were shoved up in tense stabs, relax back down.

There. It's done.

No need to worry anymore.

But part of me has to wonder: If I did the right thing, then why don't I feel good about it?

⁂

Next day, it's more of the same. Nolan and I communicate by texts, though he does invite me out for lunch. I refuse.

Finally, at the end of the day, he corners he in my office.

"Sierra," he says. "Ms. Hall. Just give me a minute, will you?"

"OK." I rise.

For whatever reason, I always feel more in control on my feet. Maybe it's because, in this case, it means I could bolt at any second.

"I screwed up the other day," he says, frowning around the words. The furrow between his eyebrows somehow makes him even sexier, damn it! "But not by what happened between us. I really like you. I'd like to see you again."

His words wash over me, warm and tempting.

"But if this messes with our jobs..." I say.

"It won't," he says. "No matter what happens between us, you'll have a job here as long as we agreed on in the contract. That I can promise you."

"Still—" I begin.

"Give me another chance," he urges me.

"I don't know if it's even that," I say. "And I'm sorry too, by the way. Going through your phone was shitty and sketchy, and I didn't feel good about it then, and I still don't now."

"Thanks." His eyes are wary, but his next grin is a smirk. "Know how you can make it up to me?"

"No." I find myself smiling too. "How?"

He takes a step forward, and my heart skips a beat. "I got us tickets to see the Red Hot Chili Peppers. Come with me."

Now my heart skips another. RHCP, holy shit—really?

Although I force myself to just say, "Nolan—"

That smile of his is indefatigable. And sexy. And yummy. "The correct answer would be: yes."

I sigh, not able to completely hold back my smile. Maybe if I have a bit of time to think about it... "When is it?"

"Tonight."

So much for time to think about it.

"Do I have to decide right this second?"

Nolan looks at his watch. "No—but let's say in an hour?"

"That sounds fair to me," I say.

I wait until he's out of the room to do an embarrassing little victory dance.

"Although you still haven't made up your mind," I chide myself quietly.

Great. Now I'm talking to myself like a kook.

Really, who am I kidding, though? Tickets to see RHCP?!? And with Nolan Storm, who's actually sorry and wants another chance with me?

Who would say no?

Although I can't totally dismiss the little ball of nerves in my stomach. I like this guy too much already. I'm already in too deep.

I end up calling him up.

"Where are you?" he asks, picking up.

"In my office, why?"

"I just thought... Why not just come and see me if you're still here?"

"Because you could be anywhere with the reno guys," I lie.

Because I can't keep my head when you're around, I mean.

"If you didn't want to look me in the eye when you rejected me, then can you just get it over with?" he jokes, although there's a pained note in his voice.

"Do you want me to reject you?" I joke back.

"Do I really have to answer that?"

"I'd like to go," I say, smile finally growing into a beam. "Tonight sounds fun."

"Well." One word and I can hear the smile in his voice too. "It just got a whole lot more fun."

**

The day speeds by while I work on the article. God, I love my job.

I send it to Nolan just before leaving.

On my way out, I run into him.

"You're leaving?" he says.

"I'm not going to the concert in this…" I say, gesturing to my very work-ish skirt suit.

"I just thought before, maybe we could grab dinner and…" He gives a little shrug. "You know what, forget it. I'll pick you up at eight?"

"Sounds good," I say with a smile, hurrying out.

I'm not about to admit that my whole body is buzzy and silly-feeling, and that dinner actually sounds amazing.

Back at my place, I've barely told Josie and Wynona about the concert before Josie blurts out, "OK, we're coming."

At my surprised silence, she groans and probably rolls her eyes. "Not to the concert, silly. To help you get ready. The video chat thing is annoying and I miss you anyway."

"It's been literally one day since we've seen her," Wynona reminds her.

"And we don't all have some lumberjack date to keep us occupied tonight," Josie snips back.

"He's not a lumberjack, he's a ranger," Wynona says in the long-suffering tone of someone who's said it all before.

"Anyway, see you soon!" Josie says.

Minutes later, she's there, bulging makeup bag in hand.

"Let's get this party started," she says.

Minutes later, Enrique Iglesias is blasting, Josie's hand is whirring away in makeup-applying expertise, and we're arguing over which outfit I should wear tonight.

"Josie," I plead with her. "That black crop top barely covers my belly button."

"Hello?" she replies. "That's the entire point of a crop top. Plus, you have a horrendously flat stomach, so I don't see what the big deal is."

"Can you just compromise with me on the red crop top?"

She sniffs. "That's not really a crop top, though. You only see a sliver of skin."

"Which I like."

In the end, I let her do a stellar smoky eye on me, and put on the red crop top. We have some Oreos, then it's time to go.

"I'll give Horatio a walk before I go," Josie offers, since she has a key to my place. "Love you. Good luck."

I muster up my most confident face as I leave. Although a big part of me is thinking I need it—all the good luck I can get.

**

The car ride there is easy. Nolan and I chitchat about nothing important, current news and stuff like that. He doesn't give me one of those inscrutable sexy looks that turn my insides to jelly, although his first look when I got into his Porsche was long and pleased enough to make an excited shiver travel down my back.

Then, all at once, we're there, at Madison Square Garden, under dancing red and white skylights, surrounded by thousands of people. The fact that Nolan got us a complete package, drinks included, isn't the first surprise I find.

"No way," I say when I find out. "You didn't."

CHAPTER 11

Nolan

"I did," I tell, grinning wide.

I can't get enough of how her pouty red lips grin when she's delighted like this.

"Front row seats?" she exclaims. "But that must've cost a…" She trails off.

I shrug, slinging my arm around her. "What can I say? It's worth it."

"Oh yeah?" she says, settling into my arm with a smile.

"Yeah," I say, placing a kiss on top of her head.

She freezes.

"Sorry," I say. "I don't want this to be weird."

"It's not, I'm sorry too," she says. "I'm just jumpy."

"Maybe we need more nachos?" I joke, indicating the bucket we already have.

"Yeah." She giggles. "That must be it."

I pick one up and pop it into her mouth. "Nacho coming right up."

Goddamn do I like seeing this girl happy.

Part of me loves making anyone laugh—girls especially—but something about how her blue eyes squeeze into delighted half-moons…

She pops one in my mouth.

"Here," I say, eyeing her and wiping a smear of cheese from the corner of her lip. "Don't want to scare the band off."

She turns and gapes as they stride on: Anthony Kiedis, Flea and Chad Smith, all of them bare-chested and grinning already.

I give her a little squeeze. "Close enough to touch, I know. They're about to start, too."

Minutes later, 'Can't Stop' is blasting into the room and we're on our feet dancing.

As Anthony Kiedis directs the chorus of the song directly to Sierra, I can't help my grip around her getting protective.

That's my girl you're singing to, buddy.

My girl—what the hell?

Although as Sierra throws her head back and grins delightedly at me, the tension in me dissipates.

"I can't believe this!" she exclaims. "This is amazing! Thank you!"

Our gazes fall on each other—meet.

Next second, our lips are meeting too. Our kiss develops along with the music as the next song starts. Her hand presses against my chest, my hands envelop her shoulders.

The next song is 'Otherside', and our kiss moves along to that too.

Fuck, she's so pretty. So perfect.

I want to take her here right here and now, crowd and concert and band be damned.

She pushes me away with a giggle. "Nolan."

I steal another kiss. "Sierra."

"I can't believe you did this for me," she says happily.

"Well," I hedge, "I am a fan of the band too, and..."

Her face falls. "Oh, sorry. Yeah, I shouldn't have just assumed..."

"Kiss me," I tell her, cupping her face in my hands.

This kiss is shyer, more hesitant.

Breaking away, I tell her. "OK, you got me. This is for you. I really meant what I said: I want to make it up to you. I want to see more of you, be more with you."

"But we work together," she protests quietly. "What are we even doing?"

The lyrics wash over us as we look at each other. Her hair is all askew, her shirt is low enough to show off her collarbone. I want to kiss every part of her.

"I shouldn't have said that." Her face falls again as she gives her head a little shake. "Why do I keep saying—"

Impulsively, my hand grabs hers. "Stop it. It's the same for me."

Her gaze lands on mine, hopeful and unsure. "What is?"

"I can't control myself when I'm with you," I growl, and next second, we're kissing again.

The rest of the concert is punctuated with more nachos, some beers, some popcorn. I can't seem to stop kissing her, holding her, taking her hand in mine. She just feels so goddamn good in my arms. I even have her sit on my lap for a bit, until she wriggles laughingly off.

Too fast, the Peppers play their last song—'Tell Me Baby'—and it's time to go. Luckily, I only had a couple of beers, so after leading us through the crowds to my car, I'm able to drive us home.

"That was…" she says, trailing off and shaking her head once we get in the car and get going. "Amazing. Thank you!"

"My pleasure," I say. "I had a great time."

And she smiles and I smile, and we sit there in silence as I drive along, because even sitting beside her doing nothing at all is better than fucking another girl.

Whoa… where the hell did that thought come from?

The next few minutes pass quickly, and next thing I know, my car is stopped in front of her place and she's about to go.

"Thanks again," she says, with a shy smile.

"You're welcome again," I say.

"You never said it once," she points out.

I grin. "C'mere."

I pull her in for a kiss, long, slow and sweet, that leaves me wanting more. Much more.

When she pulls away, she says, "Goodnight."

She's opened the car door when I say, "Wait."

She waits.

Our lips find each other, and the car door swings back closed, and the rest is what happens when you're alone in a car with tinted windows and someone who drives you mad. Someone like Sierra Hall.

She tastes so good and feels so good, I can't think of anything else.

The way her tongue teases and takes turns leading mine. How her body is pressing against mine.

When she clambers onto my seat and straddles me, I get rock-hard. She grinds herself on me.

"You tease," I growl, cupping the back of her head so I can give her neck a bite-tinged kiss.

Her breath is hot and heavy into my shoulder as my hands glide down the shape of her, the perfect hourglass swell of her. Those hips, that pussy, grinding into me.

I could take her now.

I adjust my car seat back so we have more room. Her gaze catches mine. "What's that for?"

I manage a half-smile. "What do you think?"

In the space in front of the seat, she gets down on her knees, her hands stroking my cock over my pants. "I think someone's happy to see me."

I grin. "Maybe you should see for yourself."

Her hands massage my cock some more, and a low growl rolls out of my throat.

"You think so?" she says casually.

"Sierra," is all I can growl.

She just smiles and leans up to give me a kiss as her hands undo my belt and lower my jeans.

More stroking. This time the only thing separating my bare cock from her skillful hands is my briefs. Then, all at once, her hands slip under and grasp my erection.

Fuck yeah.

"Whoa," she murmurs.

Next second, her 'whoa' is tasting my cock.

"Fuck," I growl. "You..."

She just slides her mouth up and down me, her hand stroking my base in time.

Already I'm rock-hard, ridiculously close to the edge. I never get this close this fast.

But what this woman does to me...

The way her perfect little mouth is pleasuring me... up and down... up and down... up... and all the way down, until the head of my cock mashes into the back of her throat.

She starts out sucking me slow, but soon speeds up, using her lips around her teeth to create a perfect tight seal.

When she cups my balls, throwing her head up and down my cock with her mouth and tongue and hands all stroking me in tandem, I can't take it anymore.

"Fuck," I hiss as I come, blasting into her mouth.

Smiling, eyes still on me, she swallows.

Next thing I know, she's hoisted herself back on me, riding me like a pro and moaning immediately. Within seconds, I'm hard again.

This fucking minx.

Our bodies slap together as we fuck some more.

She's close, too—the way her groaning has becoming pitched tells me that.

My hands go under her top and enjoy her breasts. My head dips so I envelop one nipple in my mouth.

"Nolan," she moans.

"Sierra," I growl.

"Fuck me harder," she pleads. "Please."

I'm all too happy to oblige, gripping her by the hips and lifting her on and off my cock in a frenzy.

Seconds later, she's coming, squirming all over me as she breaks out shaking, slumping on my front.

But I haven't had near enough of her yet. I prop her up on the car seat, then get to my knees. "My turn."

Still recovering and catching her breath, all Sierra can do is let out a low groan. I caress her thighs and she trembles. My lips pepper there with nibbles and kisses and she twists with still-sensitive pleasure.

As my lips kiss their way to her clit, my fingers tease her opening, circling round it before I insert one, then two. Until her pussy is shoved out, clasping desperately at my fingers, just as my lips land on her clit.

"Oh—Nolan!" she wails.

Too bad I'm only getting started. I lap her clit in slow sweeps just as my fingers sweep deeper inside her. Already, she's shaking, close.

"Please," she groans.

I finger-fuck her mercilessly as my tongue swirls over her clit. Seconds later, she's coming, crying out and shaking, before slumping onto the car seat.

I get on the one beside her and take her in my arms.

As I'm holding her, a random thought pops in. I wait until a few minutes have passed and she's about ready to go before voicing it, though: "Any plans tonight?"

Still naked and gorgeous, she eyes me with a faint half-smile. "Why—want to insert yourself in them?"

I'm all smiles myself. "That's not the only thing I want to insert myself in."

She gives me a playful smack. "Nolan!"

"Don't pretend that you wouldn't like that too."

She bites her lip, although her tone is stern: "You still haven't answered."

I assume a nonchalant expression. "Sure—yeah. I might like to."

"Might?"

"OK." I glare at her. "Let's sleep over at yours. Happy now?"

Her response is to give me a big kiss that wakes up my cock again. "Yes. Happy now?"

I grab my briefs and put them on. If we keep it up like this we'll never get out of this car. "Yeah, now that you mention it."

Inside her place, a little gray terror rushes to the door and barks at me until Sierra picks him up and scolds him. "Horatio!"

Although he is a cute little terror.

"Nice name," I say.

She grins. "Thanks. Mom named him after her favorite British admiral when she gave him to me for Christmas. She loved that quote: Time is everything; five minutes make the difference between victory and defeat."

"Oh yeah? And what do you think?"

She delivers me a quizzical look. "What do I think of what?"

"You really think that time is everything?"

She grins. "Maybe. Although it can't fix everything—or 'heal all wounds', as the saying goes."

I lift an imaginary glass. "Hear, hear. A girl after my own heart."

Part of me wishes I had an actual glass—of alcohol. One of the wounds time hasn't healed just decided to enter my head.

Why do I always end up talking about serious, real shit with this girl, anyway?

She just laughs. "Anything in particular you had in mind for us to do, now that we're here?"

I shrug. "Any movies you've been wanting to see?"

She glances at her phone. "Whoops, actually it's past one AM. I hate to be a buzzkill, but we should probably..."

"OK, OK, buzzkill," I say. "Sleep it is. Although you did ask."

Her smile has the graciousness to be guilty. And cute. "You can nominate me for worst hostess ever."

I smirk. "That could still be balanced out by our amazing sex."

Next thing I know, I've swept her up in my arms. "Alright. I'm ready. Show me to the bedroom."

"Yes, sir," she says with a giggle. "It's the only room straight ahead."

"Knew I'd need help finding it."

We're both laughing as we enter her room.

It's filled with pictures of her with two friends who look like twins.

Wonder if I'll ever make it into any of those pictures...

Crazy thought.

"You really have a thing for twins, eh?" I joke instead, right before I kiss her hard.

She just laughs and kisses me harder.

In bed together, under her white cotton sheets, her gorgeous naked body against mine feels so right. We make love again, then fall asleep in each other's arms.

At seven AM, my internal alarm clock wakes me up, as usual.

What isn't usual, though, is that I don't feel like sneaking out. No, this weird undefinable buzzy pit in my gut brings me into her kitchen.

The fridge is an empty white coffin, though—no eggs to make, not even any milk to pour into a cereal bowl. This whole place is almost like an Ikea display kitchen, it's so clean, empty and foodless.

Nothing, except one cupboard of...

Damn. This girl really likes her ramen.

With a shrug, I find a stainless-steel pot and a wooden ladle, dump in the package, and get cooking.

By the time I carry the steaming hot bowl into the bedroom, she's propped herself half-up, squinting at me like she can't comprehend what ramen even is.

I spoon out a bit and extend it to her. "Just taste, and you'll see."

She swallows some, and her grin widens. "You... made ramen breakfast for me?"

"There was nothing else in your kitchen," I protest, a bit more defensively than I'd like.

She just laughs, cheeks heating up. "Yeah... I... well... Thanks?"

I take a spoonful myself. "Huh. It's actually pretty good."

She giggles while I shrug and take another spoonful. "What can I say—I guess I'm a talented ramen chef too. It's a gift."

"Come into bed," is all she says, still chuckling.

So, I do.

And what I can't figure out, as I sit beside this girl in her bed, and we pass spoonfuls of ramen back and forth, is why this stupid smile on my face won't go away.

CHAPTER 12

Sierra

Today, today, today.

I lock myself in the single stall bathroom at the comedy club and grin at my rosy-cheeked reflection like an idiot.

Nolan Storm. Nolan fucking Storm.

The past 24 hours still feel like some fan-fiction the twins—OK, Wynona since she was the one who was into that—would write to taunt me.

But it actually happened. He actually took me out, took me home. Stayed the night. Made me breakfast in bed.

Red Hot Chili Peppers, nachos, amazing car sex, even better sex in bed, ramen breakfast in bed.

Is this real life?

Back in my office, as my fingers dance across the keyboard and idea after idea pours out onto the page, I keep having to resist the urge to laugh out loud like a complete crazy. But I can't help it.

Just the thought of him makes a smile start taking over my entire face.

Even if he's my boss. Even if it's not a good idea.

Screw it—it's far too late for good ideas anyway.

He steals into my office around 10 AM for a quick kiss... that ends up not being so quick.

How could it be with how good his lips feel on mine?

Seeing my expression, he draws away with a suspicious smirk. "What?"

"Just... I was thinking: right now, I'm being paid to kiss my boss."

Nolan's smirk widens as his eyes narrow. "You."

I just laugh, and we kiss again. Those two have been solutions to a lot of things lately: stress, uncertainty about this situation, speechlessness—a laugh or a kiss.

And both are in abundance with Mr. Storm.

He manages to finally tear himself away half an hour later.

An hour or so after that, at lunchtime, he strides into my office as if we hadn't spent the better part of the morning kissing and are probably all set for some more.

"What's up?" I ask him.

"Forget it," he says, not even trying to smile. "Let's just go for lunch."

"OK..." I say, although I get my things and follow him outside.

As he strides along the sidewalk, glaring at nothing, I pause. "Do I get to find out where we're going for lunch?"

He pauses. "Of course, yeah. Let's do Baltazk's."

"Sounds good to me."

We head across the street to the building with the abstract art primary color mosaic diagonally painting its exterior. Inside, the brunette waitress finds us a private table in the back that overlooks its own courtyard.

Even once we've sat down and taken a sip of our waters, Nolan looks much the same. He hasn't even picked up the menu, is glaring at one of the ugly striped abstract art prints like it personally insulted him.

"You don't have to tell me what's going on," I say, frowning myself. "But if you're going to sulk this whole time..."

He rakes a tense hand through his tied-back light brown hair, his hazel eyes narrowed. "It's my company funds. They just got frozen."

I drop the laminated menu that I hadn't even realized I was holding. "What?"

"Don't worry," he says quickly. "I'll make sure you're paid, even if the money comes from my own bank account." He grimaces, gives his head an angry shake. "I just didn't expect this so soon."

"Someone froze your funds?" I ask.

"It has to do with my dad's will," he says quietly, not meeting my eye. "I should've known the wily bastard would have something like this up his sleeve, but still." He shakes his head again, a little sadly this time. "Didn't see it coming."

"Oh," I say.

I'm not sure what else to say. Is it really my place to ask Nolan why his dad would do something like that?

Grabbing his water glass, Nolan downs it in a single breathless gulp. Then he fixes hardened, unseeing eyes on me. "I have to get married."

I was halfway through picking up my own water glass—but at that, I put it right the hell down. "What?!?"

"Forget it." Nolan picks up his menu, gives it a quick scan, then drops it. "I shouldn't be getting you involved in this."

"Telling me is getting me involved?"

"No, just..." He scowls. "Fine. It's my dad's will. He always thought I was too wild for my own good, was always wanting me to settle down. So, he put in his will that either I find myself a wife—or I find myself another inheritance." His chuckle has a note of dark irony in it. "That's Dad for you—he never went halfway with things.

Anyway, the deadline for me to find a wife is coming up soon, and I'm not going to just tie the knot for the sake of it, so..."

"Really?" I say.

His eyebrows crinkle at my tone.

"I don't know," I say. "You haven't thought of..."

"Just marrying someone for the hell of it, making sure I get a pre-nup down, then divorcing the hell out of her?" He scowls, making a face. "Of course I have." He shakes his head. "But hell, the hassle of it all, and the ethics of just messing with the system when there isn't anyone I can stand to be around for more than a few..." He trails off as his gaze lands on me.

He smiles his first smile of the hour. "You know, you just might be a genius."

Despite the circumstances, I'm still able to laugh. "Sure?"

"No." He grabs both my hands. "I mean—we could do it. You and I. I'd give you a cut, of course, but... yeah." He grins. "We could do this."

Suddenly, my hands feel limp in his, like they could drop to the floor, through the floor, even.

Did he just seize them in the spur of the moment, or to try and convince me of what he just said?

And hell, his handsome, irresistible smile, that eager light in his eyes—everything about him is convincing. So, why aren't I convinced?

"Sierra?" he says. "I know it's sudden, but..."

I rip my hands away from his. It seems like the top of my head has opened up and everything I was going to say has walked right on out of it.

I pause. There's one weird hope left—one hope that's reasonable, too. "You're serious?"

His face lights up—and in that quarter-second, my heart does a happy hop because I can almost hear it: "Gotcha! Kidding!"

Only he never says it. Suddenly, his expression goes flat.

"If you don't want to, you can just say so," he says.

Somehow the napkin got into my hand, and now I'm balling it in there, squishing it into the smallest, tiniest ball I can.

So. This is how it is for him. This is what I am to him.

"Listen," he says, reaching out a hand. "I like spending time with you. I think we could both use the money. It's a no-brainer—so why not?"

That hand of his, that hand that's held my hand, stroked my body, cupped my face, I want to take it. I do.

But I can't.

Not yet, anyway.

I rise. "I..." Where to even begin? "I'll need some time. To think about this."

Nolan nods, head down like a dog that's been scolded. "So... tonight, if I came over?"

My hand on the cool metal of the chair, I look at him sadly. "You don't get it?"

He grabs his water, before remembering there's nothing left to drink. He frowns at me, like I'm to blame for it. "Get what?"

I could laugh out of sheer exasperation. "That this changes things. Didn't you consider that? That what we had was real—to me, at least—and now..."

"Now... what?" He rises too, although he leans over the table so that we'd be eye to eye if he wasn't a good foot taller than me. "Why can't it be like before, except we're fake engaged and we make a killing out of it? What's wrong with that?"

Now I do laugh, and the laugh that comes out of me is exasperated, frustrated, sad. "Other than lying to our family and friends? Other than me going out with a guy like I'm some paid... I don't know, escort? Other than..."

"OK, OK," Nolan says wearily. "You got me at the lying part. But that last bit—I thought, you don't have fun with me?"

"Yes." I shrug. "So?"

"So, it wouldn't like you were a..." He scowls, unwilling to even say the word. "I mean, if you'd want to go out with me normally, now, it's practically the same, except we'll get an even bigger benefit than most couples."

I stand there.

His words twist in me like a fishing hook I willingly swallowed: A bigger benefit than most couples.

All around us is pleasant conversation, ugly abstract bleh-colored paintings. Someone's ordered a stinky fish dish, someone else is wearing perfume that smells like a perfume store exploded.

I stand there and wait for Nolan to get it, until it dawns on me that he doesn't, won't ever.

No, he won't ever get it, because it hasn't been the same for him.

Maybe it just hasn't been real for him the same way it has been for me.

"You really don't get it," I finally say, like an idiot.

"So, that's a no?" he asks. His arms are two impotent hulks at his side. "Jesus, Sierra. You could've just said no. I never wanted to pressure you into anything. I just didn't think it was a big deal."

Suddenly, I'm sick to death of myself. Of this whole situation. Of me waiting around here for him to catch on in a way he clearly isn't going to.

"I've got to go," I say.

He catches me by the arm. "Don't be like that. Let's just talk this over, and—"

"I don't want to talk this over." God, I could slap him right now. "I want time to think. Alone."

His hand slumps down.

For once, Nolan Storm doesn't have a cheeky or assholish reply.

"I'll finish up the article at home," I say as I head out. "Goodbye."

**

"Well," Wynona says meditatively a few hours later, as she uses a little applicator to add tiny black cats to her neon green toenails. "There is the money."

"Oh, shut up, you," Josie says, shaking her popcorn-filled hand at her sister. "Sierra's dignity is worth more than all the money in the world."

Wynona looks up to eye me head-on. "But is it dignified to be eating ramen for the rest of your life?"

I glare at her, grabbing an ample handful of popcorn for myself. "Maybe. I don't know. Anyway, this job should keep me going for another few months at least."

"But with the kind of money you'd be getting from marrying Nolan Storm, you could be set up for years," Wynona crows, eyes bulging at the last word. "Maybe even decades. We could finally go to Italy."

Mouth full of popcorn, Josie lifts her pink-nailed hand. "Hello? Poor twin still here. Anyway, it's not our job to pressure Sierra—it's our job to support her no matter what choice she makes."

Wynona just rolls her eyes. "Thanks, Dr. Josiecorn. But I'm with Nolan here. What's the big deal if you like him already?"

The blue pastel macaroon-printed Kleenex box that Josie chucks at Wynona barely misses her by an inch.

"You bitch!" Wynona cries, although she makes no move to get up—she's still not done with her nails.

"The deal," Josie says coolly, "you heartless whore, is that now it's more like he's using her."

Now it's my turn to raise my hand. "Hi. This is my life we're talking about. I'm here and can speak for myself, thank you."

"No, no, no," Wynona says to Josie, ignoring me. "Why can't it be both? He likes her and they have a mutually monetarily beneficial situation they're involved in?"

"Because it's not that simple," I say quietly.

And suddenly, finally, both twins shut up and look at me. It's clearly my turn to speak.

"Because if he really thought we had something," I say, "would he really have brought up the whole fake engagement thing at all?"

"No," Josie says, at the same time that Wynona says, "Yes."

I just shrug. "You guys weren't there. That other night, when we went to see the Peppers, and slept over at my place, it was magical.

We danced, sang, kissed, you know. But now, it's like it's... tainted somehow. Like it doesn't mean as much as I thought it did. If he's willing to entangle it with this whole inheritance trouble of his." I move a single half-smushed popcorn around my palm, wanting to eat it, crush it, throw it. But I just move it, the kernel part scrapping my skin a little. "You can't mix up real and fake like that and keep them separate—eventually they all get mixed up."

For the first time, Wynona's dark cat-eyes seem to understand the gravity of the situation, as she says: "The real question is: will the fake become real, or the real fake?"

CHAPTER 13

Nolan

Bounce…

…Bounce

Bounce…

…Bounce

"Shut up!" Jax yells from inside the guest bedroom.

"You shut up!" I yell back.

"It's 11 at night!"

"Yeah—it's 11 at night! And this is my place!"

He stalks out, grabbing the tennis ball I'd been bouncing against the wall out of the air. He gives it a shake. "Why?"

"Why not?"

"Because I'm trying to sleep!"

"Dude. It's a Friday night."

"And? Laura won't answer my calls, you don't want to go out, and—"

"Oh. So this is my fault now, that you're being a teen girl and want to go to bed at a laughable hour on a weekend? Actually, scratch that—teen girls love to stay up late."

Jax chucks the tennis ball into the kitchen sink. "Whatever. Just cut it out."

"Or?" I'm lazy enough to not stalk over to the sink and grab the tennis ball to make my point, but I still have enough energy for some petty, pointless fighting. "What? You'll leave my place?"

Jax just glares at me, crossing his freckled arms over his bare chest. "Dude. Not my problem that the stopwatch is ticking down for your dad's will thing, and that you haven't found your boo."

"It is your fault if you keep me from my one and only love."

"Being an annoying fuck?"

I chuck a couch pillow at him, which he catches. "Dude."

"Dude."

"What about that girl you've been seeing?" he asks.

"Which one?" I ask, contemplating another couch cushion crashing into his head.

"The one who's had you smiling like a wiener these past few days."

I scoff. "Fuck off."

Jax has the observational skills of a potato. No way did he notice something like that.

I must've given it away, somehow.

Jax chucks the couch pillow at me. I catch it.

"Fine," I tell him, throwing myself upright before I can think better of it. "We'll go out, you and I. A wild night on the town in our city that never sleeps. Happy?"

He tries to fight the beginnings of a smile, without success. "I'll be happy when I have a few Guinesses in me."

I give him a big clapping pat on the back. "That's more like it, my man."

Come to think of it, that's probably what I need too: enough alcohol to forget my name, and enough women to forget Sierra.

She still hasn't responded to any of my texts.

I'm probably kidding myself about the women part. Even just trying to dial up one of my usuals had me chucking the phone across the room in frustration earlier today. But at least alcohol would drown out the memories of Sierra and I replaying in my head. Like those fucking YouTube ads they won't let you skip until 30 seconds have passed or you piss away money on their Premium bullshit.

I can't seem to get it out of my head: the face she wore after I brought up the stupid fake engagement thing—the one I'd never seen before and don't much care to ever see again. A mix of looks I can't place. Confusion was in there somewhere, and hurt.

I hurt her.

"Jax," I say, suddenly. "What would you say if all we had to do was get fake married and you'd get a shit-ton of money?"

"Fuck off," he says, deadpan.

"I'm not joking."

Seeing his horrifically grimaced face, I add quickly, "I'm not serious. Just—if you were a girl, and you were dating me, and—"

Jax just shakes his head, still grimacing. "Dude. This is way, way too far from my current existence."

"Forget it," I say, scowling.

I was stupid even bringing it up.

But I can't get it out of my fucking head. How, somehow, bringing it up to Sierra—a perfectly reasonable suggestion—I ruined something. Broke something that can't be put back together again.

Fucking women.

I would rather not have said it and gotten to see her tonight.

I could've gone over there, or she could've come over here... I could've booted Jax and hooked him up at one of my buddies' places, gotten Sierra and I this place for ourselves for the night—or maybe taken her out to one of those hot new rooftop pool clubs I keep hearing about...

"Hello?" Jax is waving a sunburned hand in front of my face. "Are we going this century?"

"You really need to get on that sunscreen bandwagon," I say, flashing him a winning smile. "I hear it can prevent sunburn."

"Yeah, yeah," Jax says, although he's smiling.

Inside the cab, though, even as Jax grumbles about how his basketball team lost the playoffs and all the reasons he should (and won't) forget about Laura (he actually mentions her vanilla-smelling hair, for Christ's sake), I can't get her out of my head.

That smile I was starting to get out of her. Like a book unfolding, it seemed to reach her changeable blue eyes more and more until— it was gone.

Will I ever see that smile again?

Fuck me, if I haven't lost my head over this fucking woman. That's it—

"Jax," I say suddenly. "If you were with a girl who was cool, one you actually liked—"

"Like Laura," he says, visibly deflating.

"Like any of the many wonderful, gorgeous women you will meet over the next few years who Laura won't hold a candle to," I say patiently.

"Anyway, would you run a fake engagement by them?" I add.

Jax, who has been gloomily watching our cab pass cars on the freeway, spins his thick freckled neck around to eye me. "Huh?"

"You know," I say reasonably. "Offer a fake engagement arrangement to the—"

"Nope," he says immediately.

"Let me finish," I growl. "Offer a financially lucrative fake engagement to them."

Jax squints at me, as if this is one of those stupid word games (Peter Piper picked a peck of pickled peppers) his cousin used to annoy us with when we were all stoned off our faces. "And I like this girl?" he asks.

"Yeah," I say. "More or—"

"Nope."

"You didn't even hear the rest of it!" I protest.

He shrugs. "Don't need to. If I actually like a girl, there's no way in fuck I'm going to propose some crazy fake engagement to her."

"But what if the need was dire, like you'd lose a lot of money if you didn't?"

"Nah."

"Dude."

Jax eyes me, shaking his head. "Dude. What dumb-ass thing did you do this time?"

"Fuck off."

He turns back to the window. "Who knows, maybe you're right. Maybe with all that money you can buy yourself a shit-ton of escorts and, with some luck, you might even like one."

"But why does it have to ruin things? Why does it have to change anything?"

Back still to me, Jax just shakes his head. "I'm not going to dignify that with a response."

"Well, can you dignify me with your credit card then, because this broke motherfucker has to pay for the comedy club renos out of pocket now."

Scowling, Jax hands it over.

A few minutes later, we've just arrived at the club when my phone goes off.

The voice is feminine but weird, all nasally and unfamiliar, and I'm thinking that whatever this chick is selling, she's doing a shit job. I'm about to snap it off, when I hear: "Emerson Storm—"

"What?" I say, shoving the phone to my ear.

"Your brother, Emerson Storm," a not-very-patient-sounding female voice says. "He had an accident. He's at Hillerston Hospital. You were his first contact."

"What accident?" I snap, stalking away from the club to hear better.

"Overconsumption of alcohol—to a near-fatal dosage," the nurse snaps, as if I were the one who poured the alcohol down his throat.

Already, I'm flagging down the cab we just got out of.

"Is he OK?" I ask Nurse Bitchy.

"Yes," she says. "But—"

"Don't say another word," I tell her, gesturing Jax in with me. "I'm on my way."

By the time we get there, I've called up Landon and Greyson. As I race into the waiting room, I see that Landon's already there.

"He's OK," he says, rising. "But asleep."

As I go to move around him, he stops me. "They won't let you see him."

"What—why?"

"Like I said, he's sleeping," Landon says, frowning. "Shouldn't be disturbed."

I freeze.

Suddenly, the adrenaline that's been spiking through my veins falls off the deep end. Tiredness is all it leaves.

"Let's go to the vending machine," Landon says. He turns to Jax. "Want anything?"

Jax, a National Geographic with a whale cover in hand, just shakes his red-haired head. "Nah."

We stalk down hallways with fluorescent lights that make my eyes hurt.

"What the hell happened?" I ask Landon.

He shrugs. "Emerson partied too hard. Can't get over this Molly chick."

"Fucking Molly," I growl.

I can feel Landon giving me a judgy side-eye. "Alright, what is it?" I ask him.

"Where were you?"

"What do you mean, where was I? I didn't even know Emerson was at a fucking party, OK? And last time I called and checked up on him a few days back, he was fine. Where were you?"

Landon stops suddenly, and it takes a few seconds for me to realize why. The vending machine. Right.

"You're right," he says. "I just... this is fucked. Messing with my head." He leans against the wall, and I wonder if he sees how eerie this place is.

Not that this hospital is any different from any other. It's eerie in the same way I've always found hospitals eerie: too clean, too white, and filled with people who seem like ghosts.

"You really don't get it, do you?" he's saying now.

This is the second time I've heard those words tonight. And yet, no, I really don't fucking get it.

"You gonna tell me?" I growl. "Dear twin?"

His hand on the wall forms a fist. "It's not some fucking joke, Nolan. You got him into partying. Emerson looks up to you—and he partied himself nearly to death just now."

"Whoa." I spin to glare at him. "You're not pinning this on me."

"I'm not—but Christ." Head hung, Landon's voice is hoarse. "We almost lost him."

I sink to the wall, to the floor as it sinks over me. What I haven't really considered since I got that call.

We really almost lost him. My baby brother. Emerson.

Fuck.

"You're right," I say. "We need to look out for him. I need to look out for him. I'll have him move in, and…"

Landon just sinks beside me. "Emerson's always been the good kid. The baby. I think losing Dad, and then this Molly chick…"

I nod. "Dad dying threw everything off balance." I nudge him. "I mean… look at you. Hell, you're…"

"I'm what?" Landon can't even smile.

"You're a goddamn husband. A dad."

"Yeah, and?"

"It's just big, is all."

"It's my life."

As I toss him a sidelong glance I don't think he notices, what I see on his face surprises me. It's not the increased weariness I've noticed on him since he's gotten himself a family. Or even frustration at me that I don't really understand the stage of life he's at now.

Right now, the only thing on his face is a quiet, self-evident satisfaction.

It's weird, seeing it like this, right in front of me, so clear that I couldn't deny it even if I wanted to.

Because he is, damn it, my crazy twin brother really is happy with that family and wife of his.

Maybe—probably—marriage and all that isn't for me. But I think if I were just about any other man seeing that look on my twin brother's face, well, it'd make me a believer.

"I'll talk to him," I say, rising. "And I'll cut down on the partying."

That seems to satisfy Landon. He nods as he rises. "I'll talk to him too."

We spend the night in the waiting room.

**

The next morning, I'm more relieved than anything. Emerson is fine, doesn't even remember what dumb-ass thought or party prompted him to drink so goddamn much.

He's conscious enough to listen patiently to my attempt at a concerned big brother talk before politely telling me to go away.

Despite my offer and Emerson's own protests about not being a kid anymore, Landon insists on having him stay at his and Kyra's place for the next few weeks.

While I want to stop by for another talk, apparently tonight is some family games night for Landon, Kyra & Co., plus Greyson is already stopping by.

So, I leave it for now. I've got the whole next few weeks to bother my baby brother with rants about the benefits of sober and love-free living.

At work, there's more bad news. The renos are even further behind than we thought, which means… you guessed it: more money to piss down the Renovation Drain.

I don't realize that I've been looking forward to seeing her until I do.

Blue sunflower-covered dress, and the kind of smile that could save a day, and that's all it takes. I'm smiling.

Maybe, just maybe, today can be saved.

There are about ten different things in my head I want to say all at once, like:

You look pretty.

I'm sorry.

I take it all back.

Forget I ever said anything.

Lunch?

Any plans tonight?

Can you forgive me?

But, before I can say anything, she says, "Alright. I'll do it."

CHAPTER 14

Sierra

He blinks. "You'll do it."

God, those hazel eyes of his could lead someone off a ledge. Hopefully I'm not the one walking off one now.

"Yeah," I say. "You were right. Not a big deal."

"I was—I mean I am?"

One thing I've picked up from Josie and Wynona sometime or another: if you have no clue what you're doing, one good strategy is to smile. So, I do.

"You're the boss around here," I say before I walk away, smiling.

It feels good—having the last word, saying quotables like I'm some badass instead of one confused mess of emotions. Walking off as if it didn't take every little last iota of self-control I have.

As if just being in the same room as him didn't involve a gravitational pull stronger than any I've ever known.

Still, I do it.

I ignore how the look he's giving me might be construed as confused, maybe even apologetic, and I go back to my office to get to work. After all, that's what he hired me for.

Although when I get back to my office, ignoring the half-hearted "Hey, Sierra" he calls after me, I find another nice surprise.

"This might just turn out to be my best week in a long while," I murmur to myself as I eye the email.

**

That evening, I get to the cafe early, wearing the pinstripe gray and navy blazer the twins agreed was professional without being over-the-top, paired with the plain black pants Win thought were yawn-worthy and Josie thought were perfect.

Only time will tell.

I scan the cafe for my potential boss-to-be, although it isn't easy to stay on task.

My gaze keeps straying to furry balls of cuteness. One tabby is pawing at someone's computer cord, while a fluffy gray with green eyes is flopped in the middle of the floor like he owns the place.

"Cat cafe? The guy's a weirdo," Wynona declared morbidly as soon as I told them.

But maybe he just really likes cats?

Besides, with this interview being for a journalist position—an actual, honest-to-goodness journalist gig—I'm not going to find fault even if he wants me showing up in hot dog galoshes and playing the banjo.

There's two shaggy-haired teens sniggering over something weird on their phone who can't be Maurice. An old woman in the corner with three cats on her lap and a spoon in her bright red bun who can't be Maurice. A man close to me frowning with a scandalized face at a nearby black cat who can't be Maurice.

Which leaves... the fifteen-year-old braceface behind the counter?

"Miss Hill," someone says, and I turn around.

Huh. So much for the frowning guy not being Maurice.

Although his disgusted scowl barely makes way for a simper as he sticks out his hand, it has to be him. "I'm Maurice Howells. A pleasure."

"Nice to meet you," I say, with my best firm-but-not-too-firm handshake.

His hand is as cold and clammy as old ham. He smells painfully clean, as if he bathed in Mr. Clean instead of regular old water.

Or maybe my nerves are just sending my observational skills into overdrive?

No sooner has my butt hit the chair, then he begins. "So. You're a journalist?"

I nod. "Yep. Four-year-degree."

He sips at his fruity-looking drink like he doesn't trust the contents, but he keeps one eye on me.

"Tell me more" he says, and, as I rhyme off my various experiences, contributions and qualifications, his scowl darkens, until he sneezes, then curses. "Damned cats."

My look must have been more quizzical than I intended—after all, I hadn't heard of 'The Incatredible Cafe' until he invited me here—because he draws himself up and explains, rather officiously, "It's the closest place to my house."

"Oh," seems to be the only appropriate response here.

"Pay is a thousand a week," he says, as if it's of no consequence.

But then he puts two pudgy, hairy elbows on the table and leans over. When he opens his mouth, he blasts me with Listerine breath that doesn't seem to go with his yellowed Stongehenge-esque teeth. "And what about Nolan Storm?"

I blink.

Yep, this would qualify as my weirdest interview ever—even beating out the one Dunkin' Donuts guy who started crying about his dead beta fish and the man from TGI Fridays who berated me for not 'having more fun' in my life for refusing to accompany him on an impromptu weekend trip to Lollapalooza.

"You do know him," he insists. "Right?"

"Yes," I say.

He nods. "You're working for him. I read your article. It was good."

I smile. "Thanks."

He sweeps his arm across the table. "I don't want anything like that."

"OK…"

Another sip of his fruity drink that turns into a slurp—he must be at the end of it. "Nolan Storm is a…" His mouth contorts and the word he settles on doesn't seem like the one he was going to say: "Enigma. He doesn't give interviews to anyone. Unlike his brothers, he hasn't given a single one in four years. I want you to do a story on him. I'll give you three months to do it."

I gape at him, while in my head I do the math. One thousand a week, times three months is… holy shit.

Twelve thousand dollars?!?

"I really don't need that much time—" I begin. I almost feel bad, taking that much money for an article that probably won't take more than a couple of weeks, tops.

But the man just shakes his beret-hatted head stubbornly, as if I'm asking for a raise. "That's the price I'm offering. The question is, will you do it?"

I've never been one to set a huge amount of store in the whole 'gut feeling' thing. After all, it was my mom's gut feeling that got her with my ass of a dad. As a kid, it was a Peyton fav, with her citing 'gut feeling' as the reason why she did such things as smack me for no apparent reason at all, and throw my sparkly snow Polly Pocket down the sewer.

But, right now, I'm having a real gut feeling.

Maybe it's the cat cafe this man clearly sees as his own personal hell, maybe it's the money he's offering me for the story. Maybe I'm just being judgmental.

But something about this guy is way, way off. And it's not just that ugly pea-green beret.

"I don't know," I say.

He rises, waving his hands and sticking out a card. "You don't have to. Think about it. Give me a call."

And then he hustles out of there, leaving me standing with his professional-looking card clasped between two fingers like it's a banana peel or a bomb. I pause, take a look around.

What do you do when you're left alone in a cat cafe? Why, you get a nice latte and a fat tortoiseshell cat to pet, of course.

**

I'm almost at my door when Nolan calls.

"Guess what," he says.

"What?" I say.

Part of me's hoping he's called the fake engagement off, called my bluff. If it is a bluff, even.

"I'm taking you out tonight."

So much for him calling it off—although I am still smiling.

"Is that a good silence, or a bad silence?" he asks.

"Why can't it be both?" I reply.

"Why, aren't you just a ray of sunshine. Picnic tonight under the stars?"

"And if I have plans?"

"Invite them along—they'll have a blast."

I can't help it—I crack up. "You really are incorrigible, you know that?"

"I've been called worse."

"Yeah, well I still haven't said yes yet," I point out.

"You haven't said no either."

I sigh. "Fine. What time?"

"Don't get too excited now."

I make my tone sugar-sweet. "I can still say no, you know."

"You. You'll be the death of me."

Damn it, I can't stop laughing. "What time, Nolan?"

"Why not now, Sierra?"

"You are not coming over right now."

"And if I were?"

"Then you'd have to wait outside while I get ready."

"Outside, as in outside your room?"

"Outside, as in outside in your car."

"You're a tough one, I'll say that much," he finally says.

"And you're unbelievable! What if I had said no?"

"Then I would've headed over to the very quality pizza joint beside your place, bought myself a pity pizza and gone on home."

"You can still do that, you know. Don't let me stop you."

Now he's the one laughing. "See you at nine then?"

"Nine works," I say, and I find I'm smiling.

That's the thing about Nolan Storm: love him or hate him, he sure knows how to make me smile.

**

Nine o'clock doesn't seem to come fast at all, at least not at seven, when I'm cleaning my room. But then my clock skips clean over eight, and before I know it, I'm racing outside to his Porsche.

"You aren't exactly a prompt one, are you?" he says, wearing a stern expression.

I stick out my tongue and he grins.

Inside his car, he has an actual picnic basket.

"What?" he says, as he starts driving and I just smile at him.

The top is down and the cool wind can't decide which way to whip our hair, so it's whipping it all ways.

"You really went for it," I say. "The whole picnic thing."

"Oh no." Nolan shakes his head, his long light brown strands streaming even more wildly in the breeze. "I've always had a picnic basket and matching tulip utensil set."

I lift up the top and—sure enough, tulips galore—crack up.

Nolan snaps the top closed before I can make out anything, though. "No peeking."

"Or what?" I say.

His smirk tugs up one side of his mouth. "Our we'll have dessert first."

"Doesn't sound so bad to me."

Excitement flickers in his gaze. "Oh yeah?"

Next second, the car's barreling to the side, and his lips are on mine.

I pull away, breathless. "Nolan!"

His smirk is pure irreverence. "You said it didn't sound so bad to you."

God those lips of his, that grin… I rip my gaze away. "Is this your way of saying that you cheaped out with dessert?"

"Did I cheap out with dessert…" Nolan scoffs. He flips open the picnic basket and shoves it under my nose. "This look like cheaping out to you?"

"Oh." Would you look at that. A mini red velvet cake with an ornate S in blue icing on the top, surrounded by sunflowers. Like my dress earlier today. "No. Not at all."

He shuts it. "Yeah. Well."

We drive along in silence.

"Sorry for assuming the worst," I finally say.

"Seems like you've been doing that a lot lately," he replies sharply.

It takes a few seconds for his words to land, and my response to take off. "Yeah, because it's completely normal—bringing up a fake engagement."

He glances my way. "What about us has ever been normal to you?"

I frown. Big words that still manage to skirt around the real issue.

"So, that's it?" I ask. "You're not even going to address it?"

He shrugs. "I offered to drop it. You said you're in."

"I am, just..." I sit there, feeling so wordless and useless that part of me wants to just climb out of this car right here and now, middle of the highway be damned.

I don't want to go through it again. I don't know if I even can.

I don't know if I have the words to make him see that him even considering it hurts me, makes me question everything we have, everything I thought we had.

Maybe part of it is that relationships, especially new ones, are murky waters, and I'm not comfortable enough to tell him how I really feel about us, let alone this arrangement.

So, I just sit there and let him drive us to wherever he's driving us.

Once we pull into an empty parking lot, I nod. "OK. So, you took me here to kill me."

Nolan snorts. "A waste of a lot of good food, then. Besides, I'm kind of having fun with you."

I shoot him a sidelong eyebrow raise. "Kind of?"

He grins, and kisses my check. "Alright, I am. So sue me. Now, are we going to have our picnic, or are you afraid of a little dark?"

The words "I've never had a nighttime picnic" are barely out of my mouth before he's swept around to my door and opened it.

I can't help the fluttery surprised feeling in my chest, even if Nolan scowls. "I can be a gentleman, you know."

"I think we've established that you're full of surprises," I say, mouth smiling around the words.

"Speaking of," he says, hooking his arm in mine. "What would you say to a cliff picnic?"

"I hope you're joking."

Right now, with no lights in sight and my eyes unadjusted, we're basically walking into pitch blackness, like somehow the Earth shook and dislodged us into a separate forgotten dimension, and now we're just wandering in the middle of empty space.

It keeps feeling like this with Nolan—like we're venturing into new, untrodden ground.

"C'mon," Nolan urges me, a playful note in his voice. "It only erodes a few feet a day, nothing we can't handle."

At my playful swat, he chuckles. "OK, OK. We're almost there. You'll see."

And so, I do.

Nolan was right about the cliff—kind of. There's a tottery old metal table and chairs that sit about 10 feet away from a cliff, underneath what's probably the biggest oak tree I've ever seen.

"Don't ask me the name of this place, because I don't know," Nolan says. "Couldn't point it out on a map either. I can only drive here on one road—the route our dad used to take us." In the dark, his teeth flash into a grin. "It helped him make his big speeches, the whole cliff backdrop."

"I'll bet."

We get out the picnic foods: crispy baguette, aged cheddar cheese and some charcuterie meats, some red grapes, and start eating.

It's so humid out that the air feels like it's full of skin cream. The silence is like this part of the world has earplugs on.

Everyone says that when you lose one sense, the others make up for it. But even in the dark like this, I don't feel like I've lost one sense at all. I feel like I'm finally remembering I have taste buds and nerves as they delight in every crunch, crumb and crust of the bread, savor the sharp tang of the aged cheddar and its give under my teeth, lose themselves in the smooth slip of the salami and the satisfying puncture of the red grapes.

"You like it," Nolan says.

I chuckle. "That a question?"

He shrugs. Another flash of his teeth in the night. "Depends on your answer."

All at once, I know exactly what I want to do, here and now. "Why don't you come over here and I'll tell you."

Maybe it's the night, dark enough that it's like the world itself has closed its eyelids, or maybe it's that what's done is done, or maybe it's none of those things and that, quite simply, Nolan brings out the wildness in me, but I'm suddenly so tired of being scared and unsure and suspicious.

I just want to take the now and have it take me, whatever that means.

Nolan comes over, and I rise to meet him. The only thing that makes sense next is our lips meeting, me pressing my answer into them: "I love it."

I can feel him smile against my lips. The slightest scratch of new stubble. The tautness of his sculpted body against mine, even separated by several layers of clothing.

Our lips seem to know what they'll do before we do: they sweep and pull and give, and our tongues sweep together with a rightness that doesn't feel real. It feels impossible that two people so odd and dissimilar could come together like this, for this one perfection.

Because that's what being with Nolan Storm is. He kisses me back into a tree, and cups my face so he can get more of this, more of my lips, my body. His kisses claim more of me, venture to my neck—even his teeth get a slight taste. I groan.

His hands are holding me and his lips are tasting me, and me, my hands are tangled in his hair as one moan follows the next.

And what happens next is what you do when the night's closed its eyes and the air itself is a warm soft stroke and you're with the man you could just maybe even love.

CHAPTER 15

Nolan

I thought I knew what sex was. What it felt like to make love to a gorgeous woman and enjoy it.

Turns out, I had no fucking clue.

All it takes is one kiss with Sierra for me to know that. Her lips fit with mine, her tongue too. Her hair might be the silkiest thing I've ever felt, her skin the softest.

When I kiss her, it's like someone hit my heartbeat.

I want to touch all of her at once. Kiss her. Stroke her.

Her shoulders fit in my palms and I press my lips onto her closed eyelids.

She giggles. "What's that for?"

"For tonight," I say, grinning like a fool.

But if being a fool means I get to be with Sierra, then I'll take it.

This fool loves her scent, some kind of rich fruit-nut something that doesn't have a name, that's just her. Sierra. Sierra-a-a-a.

This fool loves the feel of her, how, right now, our hips move along to the same beat the breeze seems to be blowing.

This fool wants every part of her, all of her—now.

Before I know quite what I'm doing, I've picked her up.

Her delighted laughter fills the night. "Nolan—what the hell are you doing?"

I swirl her around as she laughs and laughs. "Whatever I want to."

"You jerk!"

"You like it."

"Prove it."

"OK."

The only thing to do then is kiss her again, kiss that smile right off her face. Until it becomes a very different smile.

Smile to smile, we find our way onto the ground, onto each other. She sits on my lap and threads her fingers through my hair.

When my eyes open, I find her stroking my hair between her two fingers, her grin rueful. "I don't know if I've ever dated a guy with better hair than me."

I flick my hair over my shoulder with a flourish. "What can I say. It's a gift."

Our eyes meet. We somehow take that to mean that it's time to laughingly kiss again.

I want her, want to be inside her, and yet, I want to make this last. I'm enjoying myself too damn much.

"Know what I'm thinking?" I kiss into her ear.

"That we never had the cake?" she asks.

We chuckle, and I shake my head. "That you'd look better without your clothes on."

Her mouth forms a turned-on 'O', although her swallowing and taking a breath gives her enough time for a sassy smirk. "That one of your lines?"

"What lines?" I joke, gesturing to myself. "I just have to show up—I don't need no lines."

We both crack up at that.

"Jerk," she purrs, both palms flat on my chest, sitting on me and rolling her pelvis on me.

My cock gets even harder.

My arms link around her, and as I get up and hold her to me, I rasp in her ear, "Let me show you what this jerk can do."

Next is a scramble, clothes torn off, lips smeared and re-smeared, an accidental on-the-nose kiss. Laughing.

Until finally, she's beautifully naked and pressed up against me while I lie on the cool grass.

My hands sweep over her. They can't help it. Every freckle, mole and bone of her is perfect, perfect.

Her mussed red-brown hair just looks black in the dark, her eyes when they open a deep blue.

My hands enjoy her upturned handfuls of breasts, while her hands run along my cock.

Our eyes meet.

"Great minds think alike," I quip.

Her grin is naughty, daring, her eyes dancing as she clambers over me. "Let me show you what this great mind can do."

Never before have I laughed and gone completely hard in the same second. But I do now.

Her lowering herself on me is nothing less than the hottest thing I've ever seen.

Her smirk wobbles, then her lips part. Then she moves her hips again, and pleasure washes over me.

Damn, this girl is good.

Too good—I'm almost at the edge and we've barely started.

I grit my teeth as she sinks herself deeper onto me, my girth completely filling her tight wetness.

Hell yeah, that's the best feeling in the world.

"Nolan," she moans as she rides me like a pro.

"Sierra," I growl back.

The way her whole body's trembling, the slack intensity on her face... she's close too.

Let's see if I can get her there.

One smack of her ass, and her climax bursts out of her as she sinks onto me and I slip her nipple into my mouth.

Fucking hell is it hot.

My girl crying out like I've never heard before, as our bodies keep slapping together.

I reposition us so that she's the one on the grass now, and, her legs propped up on me, I fuck her nice and good and deep.

I start out slow, so she can somewhat recover from her orgasm, although already she's shaking.

Her eyes are closed, her face so blissful I almost want to take a picture of it. Save it somehow.

Fuck, what's with all these weird thoughts?

It doesn't matter. All that matters is the woman I'm inside now. The woman who fits me like a fucking glove.

Into her and out of her, deep, deep, and deeper inside her, I pound her. I build my speed slowly, as moans roll out of her like some sort of slowed-down song.

I could do this all day, it feels so fucking nice. Better than the best beer I had on that weird hidden isle in Haiti, better than that time I took that little pink pill Jax still won't tell me what was in, better than the time years back that Landon and I met the hot Tamil model twins who insisted that they'd been waiting all their life to find twins worthy of a foursome.

Fuck, being with Sierra redefines the word 'better', demands something more.

She's so wet and tight I can't get enough of it.

"Nolan," she groans. "Please."

Music to my ears.

"Yeah?" I say, picking up my pace.

I'm goddamn close now. Won't be able to keep this pace up much longer.

"Yeah," she rasps.

"Yeah," I growl, jackhammering her hard.

Fuck going slow and building up to this gradually. I can't put this off any longer. I want her. I want her rough and I want her now. I want her screaming out again, even more.

It doesn't take long for my wish to be granted. I can feel it as she loses it. Her pussy gets tighter, then looser, while her body shakes harder than ever and she cries out loud.

That's all I need for the climax I've been holding inside myself to break free.

Fuck.

As I blast into her, we clasp each other tighter than ever, one release.

Afterwards, she's in my arms like she belongs there.

"Are you staring at me?" she murmurs, snuggling up against me.

"Nope. Do you want me to?"

"No." She giggles. "I... You're sure no one's going to come here and find us..."

"Ass naked on the grass?" I ask, grinning. "Don't worry, if they do, I'll just tell them we're playing cricket."

"Pfft. For a twin, you're a pretty terrible liar."

"What do you know about twins, anyway?"

"I'm friends with a pair, remember? When they were kids, they used to switch places, cause mayhem. It helped that they were great liars."

"Yeah, well, maybe I'm out of practice."

She just looks at me and laughs.

I laugh too. "So. Round two?"

Sierra grins. "Really?"

"Why not?"

She snuggles in my arms. "Because my butt is cold?"

My hands go down and start massaging it. "Here, let me help you with that."

"Because we never had the cake?"

I get up, stalk over to the picnic basket, and come back with the cakes.

We sit there, eating.

"You know, this might be the nicest thing anyone's ever done for me."

When I look over, Sierra's done with her cake, her thoughtful gaze resting on me like a shy bird that might flit away any second.

"I can't say it's anything original I came up with," I admit. "Back when we were kids, it was my mom's favorite thing to do with me. She'd prepare these literal feasts, then pick some weird place we'd never been before. Tiny forests and fields too insignificant to be on maps were her favorites."

My hand finds hers and I look out into the dark night and its shadows. "That was back when Google Maps wasn't a thing, when the world seemed a lot less explored and scoured over. Anyway, I'm rambling."

When I glance at Sierra, she's already looking at me. "You don't talk about your mom much."

"Don't I?" I shrug. I toss the cake plate away like a Frisbee, wishing I could toss away what I said too.

It's always better not to bring her up.

"You know what this means?" I say to Sierra, smiling.

"What?" she says.

All I have to do is kiss her for her to understand.

**

At work the next morning, I feel like a fucking clown.

I can't seem to get pissed off at any of the things I normally do—how a few of the guys feel the need to take smoke breaks every half-hour, how the timeline for completion keeps being pushed back, like sandbags against an inevitable flood.

I keep on smiling, like I decided 'fuck it' and came to work baked today.

Guess she's just about the best joint imaginable.

Sierra Hill.

I keep popping by her office for the stupidest shit—a pen, checking we're on for lunch, just to say hello. When really, it's just for a fucking smile.

That smile of hers…

Jesus fucking Christ, I'm losing it.

When it's finally time for lunch, I'm walking her out of there when we pass by Jeremiah, who lets out a long, low whistle.

"Careful there," I say curtly. "That's my fiancee you're whistling at."

We freeze.

Holy fuck.

Did I just say that? And why did it feel natural as hell?

One look at Sierra's sadly puzzled face, though, and I know—whatever made me do it—it wasn't worth it. Not at fucking all.

Outside, the overly bright sunlight in my eyes seems something else saying I'm a goddamn idiot. As if I didn't know already.

I touch Sierra's tense bare arm. "Hey. Sorry about that. It just slipped out."

She nods. "We are doing this, after all."

"Yeah." I straighten. "We are."

The lunch doesn't go so well, after that.

Maybe Jax had a point about this whole pretending thing.

It feels too late to go back on it, though. When I try bringing it up, Sierra just looks sad, like I don't understand what we've gotten ourselves into at all.

Back at the office, Greyson calls me up.

"Long time no talk," he says.

"Right back at you, old man," I quip. "How's the old ball and chain?"

"You're on speakerphone, Nolan dearest," Harley calls out.

They crack up, while I add, "Never said it wasn't a lovely ball and chain."

"Oh, you charmer, you," she says. "Too bad I'm taken."

"Too bad is right," Greyson says with a chuckle. "Anyway, you're off speakerphone now, I was just putting away a few dishes."

"Aren't you just husband of the year," I comment.

Greyson makes a skeptical sound. "I was thinking. We're long overdue for a family dinner. Might be good for Emerson, too."

"Good idea," I say. "Where you thinking?"

"Our place?" he says. "Harley's cleaning it now, actually, and I know she's been wanting to host a dinner for some time now."

"You guys have a pool. I'm in," I say.

He snorts. "Glad the prospect of seeing family is so appealing. There is one other thing, though..."

"I won't bring any unsuitable women, if that's what you're worried about," I say.

"Landon mentioned that you're seeing someone," Greyson says. "As long as she's not clinically insane, you could try bringing her by."

"That was one girl," I protest. "One girl with undiagnosed delusions that only came out on the second glass of wine. How was I to know? One girl and I can never live it down."

I pause.

This is the part where I should probably tell him about the engagement thing. Or at least lay the groundwork so they don't all fall out of their chairs in shock when I do tell them.

But I can't seem to get the words out.

"This girl," I say. "It's getting kind of serious, actually."

"Oh?" Greyson says. "That is interesting. You sure you're not the one suffering from delusions?"

"Thanks," I growl.

"Hey, you're the self-proclaimed forever bachelor," Greyson reminds me. "Anyway, all jokes aside, I'm happy to hear it. I'm looking forward to meeting her, too."

"Yeah, I am too," I say, surprised to actually mean it. "When's the dinner?"

"Would tomorrow be too little notice?" Greyson asks.

"I'm in," I say.

"Oh, and that new article's looking great," Greyson says. "I've had a bunch of people reach out because of it already—wondering if your comedy club restaurant does employee parties, stuff like that."

"Shit. Really?"

I do what I normally instinctively avoid and usually only do once I'm drunk enough to laugh at it—dare to check my 67,678-new-email inbox.

Sure enough, amidst offers to increase my manhood, show me naughty pictures, and kindly send me $5,000,000 from Nigeria, there it is, the real jackpot: people are reaching out because of the comedy club. Sierra's article is killing it!

"Wow," I say, flipping from one to the other as a smile climbs up my face.

"I know," Greyson says. A crash sounds in the background. "I better go—I think that was Harley with the cereal. But see you tomorrow."

"See you," I say.

I head over to Sierra's office. I pause there for a minute, peeping in her door window like a fucking weirdo. But I can't help it.

She's extra beautiful like this, all deep in concentration at her work. Her gaze is rapt on the screen, her small fingers dancing over the keyboard. Her lips purse every so often. That collarbone-skimming hot pink blouse and tight knee-length skirt aren't helping me tear my gaze away either.

Suddenly, she stops, and it takes me a few seconds to realize why—she's noticed me.

"Sorry," I say, coming in. "I didn't want to disturb you. I can come back, if you'd like."

"No, it's fine." Her smile seems proprietary. "I was just finishing up. What did you need?"

"Other than another night with you?" I quip.

When her giggling seems weak, I soldier on: "I just wanted to congratulate you on your latest article. It's really turning things around for the restaurant. I've already got a bunch of emails from prospective customers. Thank you. You're doing a great job."

Her shy smile goes wide. "Thanks. I'm really enjoying the work here."

"Keep it up," I tell her.

It feels foreign to me, this part of the job. I've managed construction projects before, and mainly my job consisted of finding ways to get the guys to want to do their jobs, and reaming out the ones who would come up with every excuse in the book as to why they had to stand around and do fuck-all for six out of eight hours a day.

"There's one other thing," I continue. "It's not really work related."

"I think I'm going to take tonight for myself," she says carefully.

"Not about... what I said before," I say, although disappointment twists in me. "It's about tomorrow night—you free?"

"I could be," she says.

"It's my brother," I say. "He's hosting this family dinner thing and I'd like you to come along."

She eyes me steadily.

Damn it, those blue eyes look a different color every time I see them. Though no matter their shade or expression, she always looks pretty as hell.

"It's for the fake engagement thing?" she says.

"No, I…" I scowl. I hadn't even been thinking of that, just now. Though Sierra does have a point. "Well, maybe we should mention it then, yeah. But I do just want you there… just because."

She nods. "Sure. Sounds good."

"Don't get so excited you fall over," I grumble.

"I'm just trying to get a handle on this, is all," she says, not quite looking at me.

"What's there to get a handle on? We like each other, are seeing each other, and are fake engaged."

"Right." She nods. "Sounds good."

She glances at me—That it?

Fuck if I know.

Lately, when I'm around her, I can't seem to get my head on straight.

"Alright," I say, before I do or say anything else stupid. "See you tomorrow night, then."

"Anything I should know about a dress code?"

I shrug. "Dress nice." Then stalk out of there.

Fuck it, if she wants to go all cold, then let her.

I'm just trying to get a handle on this—as if this whole situation is some raging bull that could gore either one of us at any second.

Although if I were honest with myself, I'd admit that I don't have a handle on it at all.

CHAPTER 16

Sierra

I sit in my office very still for a good minute or two. Then, my phone rings.

"Hello?" I say.

"Of course you haven't heard," Peyton says.

Only with my sister can I hear a sneer over the phone.

"I'm at work, Pey, can it wait?"

"Yeah, totally, I mean it's only our mother, right?"

"What are you even talking about?"

"She's at Holiday Inn. Part of her house burned down."

"What?"

"If you're too busy, though…"

I resist the urge to chuck my phone across the room. Talking to Peyton longer than 0.2 seconds often has that effect.

"Which Holiday Inn is she at?" I snap.

"The one on Lilywort Ave," she snaps back.

"What room number?"

"603."

"And she's OK?"

"Well, obviously, she's upset, but otherwise, yeah, she's fine, and—"

I hang up.

On my way out, I stop by Nolan's office. His eyebrows go up in pleased surprise.

"I have to go see my mom," I tell him. "There's been a fire."

He jumps up too. "She OK?"

"Yeah, apparently she's at a hotel with my sister. But I need to be there for her right now. I can make up the lost time a few nights next week."

"Don't worry about it," he says. "You do what you need to. But Sierra?"

"Yeah?"

"Want me to come with you?"

I hesitate. That was the one thing I didn't expect him to say.

"No, it's fine," I say, forcing a smile. "She doesn't even know I'm dating you, to be honest. So, it might be… distracting."

"Right." He nods. "Yeah. Of course, no big."

I head for the door.

"You sure?" he asks.

I throw a hand over my shoulder. "Bye, Nolan."

And as I rush to the car, I can't say why, but part of me wanted him to insist on coming.

I drive to the Holiday Inn like a maniac who doesn't want to get caught by the police. I watch my rear-view mirrors like a hawk, and weave through traffic like a snake.

My hammering heartbeat seems connected to the gas pedal, keeps revving it up higher and higher.

Only once I've pulled into the packed parking lot do I stop to take a breath.

"She's fine," I tell myself. "It's just her house, she's fine."

Though really, I know I won't be able to relax at all until I see her myself.

I hurry upstairs without so much as a token smile at the concierge so she can see I'm not a crazy person. Too damn bad. This is my mom we're talking about.

I find her in her room, sitting on the edge of the paisley-print bed, face aghast. Seeing me, she brightens. "Sierra."

I rush into a hug with her. "Mom. Thank God you're OK."

"Oh, I don't know..." She lets out a weak chuckle. "Your mother is an idiot, Sierra."

"Don't say that."

Her silver head is hung, her lips turned down in a miserable expression. "But it's true—wait until you hear how the fire started."

"I'm sure it wasn't your fault."

"I was burning some of your father's old things in the back yard— finally getting rid of the things," she recounts, scowling. "I stepped away for a second, then the fire got out of control, caught on the main house, and then..."

"Did the firefighters manage to put out the fire?" I ask.

"Obviously," Peyton says, sipping whatever latte she got from downstairs. "It wasn't a forest fire or anything like that."

I take a few seconds to consider pointing out Peyton's own stupidity to her—of course it wasn't a forest fire, it was a house fire— then dismiss it. Right now, Mom is the most important thing, not petty squabbling with my bitch of a sister.

"The whole back extension of the house is burned down," Mom says hollowly. "Gone."

"But your insurance..." I say.

She just shakes her head sadly. "I cheaped out. Figured I'd never had a fire before, so why bother being prepared for one. I'm going to have to pay for it out of pocket. But I don't have the money. Probably won't for years. I'll either have to live with a giant hole in the back of my house, or move."

"No," I say. "No way. You love that house. Me and Peyton, we can—"

"Um, the stock market hasn't been doing great lately," Peyton grumbles. "And who do you think paid for this hotel?"

I wheel around on her. "What?"

She gives her blonde-haired head a toss, pouting. "Just that, just because Harvey and I drive Cadillacs and live in a mansion, does not mean that we're just made of money with unlimited pockets."

I gape at her, before it turns into a glare. "You're not serious."

"Your sister is overextended as it is," Mom says, with a wave of her hand. "But I'll be fine. Don't you worry."

"No," I say. "You know what? You're right. We don't need to worry. Because I'm going to help you."

Mom eyes me dubiously. "But, Sierra, you just got this new job, and—"

"Yeah, and I didn't tell you, I nabbed another one too. It's high paying. I won't be able to cover all the repairs, but we can probably get an independent contractor to do some of it, or at least close that hole."

Yeah, no way am I letting my mom live with a giant hole in her house.

I go into the other room to call up Maurice.

"I have some requirements, though," I tell him. "I'm not doing anything prying or lying or negative on Mr. Storm."

"What gave you that impression?" he crackles over the phone, although he sounds grumpy. Who knows, maybe that's just the way he is. "That works for me, in any case. We can meet up every few weeks for progress reports."

"Sounds good," I say, even though it doesn't.

If I never saw the creepy guy again it would be too soon, but then again, money is money.

**

I stay over with Mom that night, and even offer to stay the next day, but she shoos me away. "Pat is coming over, I'll be fine. Plus, you have a job to get to. And don't you think about spending all of tomorrow night here. Pat's taking me out for dinner, and I don't want you hanging around here when you have your own life to live."

At work, I've barely stepped through the door when Nolan's on me. "Hey. How is she?"

"She's fine. Upset, of course. But not hurt at all, at least."

"And her place? Did they put out the fire in time?"

I manage a bitter laugh. "Depends on your definition of 'in time'. Mom lost the back part of her house, but I guess at least the whole thing didn't burn down."

"Damn." Nolan frowns. "I'm really sorry."

"It's OK," I tell him. "I'm just glad she's not hurt."

"You still up for tonight?" Nolan says. "It's OK if you're not."

I shrug. "Mom has her own plans for tonight, so I guess I'm game. It'll be a nice distraction. I might not exactly be the life of the party, though."

"Well." Nolan flashes a winning smile. "Tonight's not exactly a party, so that sounds perfect to me."

He squeezes my hand.

"OK," I say.

I squeeze his hand back.

"OK," he says. "Well."

He steals a kiss, then pulls away. "I should get to work."

"Me too," I say.

Neither of us make any move to leave.

He grins. "You first."

I grin. "No, you."

"Get a room, you two!" one of his guys calls as he passes.

Nolan just chuckles, his arms wrapping around me, as he eyes me sternly. "Alright then. Time to get to work, you."

"You're not making it easy on me," I point out.

"Me?" he protests. "What about you, wearing those high heels and thigh-high tights like that?"

I lean in, on tiptoe, so our lips are nearly touching: "Oh yeah? And what are you going to do about it?"

He steals a kiss, then pulls away. "Send you to work. Like a good boss."

I chuckle, heading off with a wave over my shoulder. "On it, boss."

The rest of the day goes by in a blur. I fill in just Josie once I get home, since Wynona's off on a date with her woodsman.

"Do you think your mom would want a care basket?" Josie asks.

"If it has your signature gingerbread cookies, then yes," I tell her. "You can drop off a couple here too."

Josie chuckles. "You pig. Anyway, I thought you had a dinner to get to."

"I do." Realizing that I've been unconsciously chewing on the inside of my lip, I force myself to stop. "God, I'm meeting his family, Jos."

"He must really like you!" she singsongs.

"I don't know," I say. "He says the fake engagement might come into play. This dinner could just be so that us being engaged comes off as believable to his family."

Josie takes a skeptical crunch of whatever she's eating. "And the picnic? And him offering to come help out with your mom? That was all for show too?"

"I don't know," I protest. "I'm just trying to take it day-by-day at this point. Although I accepted that job with that weirdo."

"No good can come out of any job with a cat hater," Josie says stoutly.

"You don't even have any cats," I point out.

"Regardless," she says.

"Yeah, well, I'm in a bit of a bind here. I can't have Mom with a hole in her house for months on end. This way, I can earn enough that we can afford to patch up the back."

"I still can't believe Peyton is broke," Josie comments. "Guess it makes sense, all those designer clothes and handbags, her and her fiance jetting off to a different resort every other weekend."

"She picked a fine time for it," I say drily. "Though who knows, maybe they've been overextended for years. Peyton's never liked living within her means."

"Well, at least your mom has you," Josie says.

"And you," I say. "Those cookies are yummy enough to make up for any pain she's feeling."

Josie chuckles. "You make them sound like Valium."

"Well, you never have told me the secret ingredient, so…"

Josie laughs some more. "OK. But aren't you just putting off getting ready at this point?"

"Yeah, probably," I admit.

"Then go! Get ready for your dinner."

"Don't say it like that," I grumble, though I'm grinning despite myself.

"Sure thing—enjoy your dinner," she simpers.

"Screw you."

"Love you."

It takes way longer than reasonable to find an outfit. Everything either makes me look like a fat nun or a skinny slut. Finally, I settle on a turtleneck dress and head out to Nolan's car.

When I get in, he doesn't say a word.

"Uh, hello?" I say, but his eyes are still on my body.

"Did I…" I begin.

"You look great," he says.

"OK," I say.

"OK," he says, peeling his gaze off me with difficulty. "Listen, about tonight. It's really not a big deal. My family's pretty chill, although my brothers can be annoying sometimes."

"It'll be weird seeing your twin there," I say.

"Why?" Paused at a stoplight, Nolan nudges me in the side. "Afraid you'll mix us up?"

"Oh yes," I say in a put-on terrified voice. "I've had nightmares about it."

Nolan just chuckles. "You'll see. We still look alike, yeah, but our hair is different. Plus, he'll be the one mooning over the brunette."

"You don't like her?"

Nolan considers this. "No, I like Kyra fine. She's good for Landon, really, she and Madison. Just... after he hooked up with her, he changed... a lot. Hardly has time for anything anymore and I rarely see him. Plus, marriage seems like a sham game."

"Says the man who's getting engaged."

"Fake engaged," he says, stabbing out his finger for emphasis.

I don't know why, but something in me folds into itself at his words.

Still, I can't stop myself from pressing, "So, you don't believe in marriage?"

A glance over finds Nolan's hazel eyes darkened, his jaw set. "Not from what I've seen of it. Sure, my brothers are happy now, but..." He shrugs. "Who knows."

A few minutes later, we pull up to a stucco Spanish-style house that's blooming with tropical plants of every kind.

"Harley has a bit of a green thumb," Nolan explains. "How she finds time to do it between her cinematography and raising little Dakota is beyond me, but she does. This is her and my brother Greyson's place, by the way."

The door opens to showcase a smiling blonde. "Hey! And don't worry, all the kids are with our favorite babysitter, who also happens to be my best friend—Hannah."

"Phew." Nolan wipes imaginary sweat off his forehead. "I was having nightmares about that."

She chuckles, glaring at him, before her green-eyed gaze lands on me. "Hey! I'm Harley." She sticks out a tan hand.

"Sierra," I say.

"You must be an interesting sort, to have caught the eye of our Nolan here," she says, grinning. "He's an oddball, that's for sure."

I laugh. It's odd, but being around Harley reminds me of kindergarten, like we could talk about just about anything. "You don't know the half of it."

Inside, giant-leaf pothos frame the entranceway. Harley strides down the hallway barefoot, her bohemian faded blue and orange lily-print robe fluttering behind her. "Greyson! They're here."

"You're the last to arrive, Nolan," Greyson says, coming down a staircase that's wound with ivy.

Nolan just shoots him a winning smile. "Last to arrive—and first to get this party started! Greyson, this is Sierra, my girlfriend."

I swing him a questioning look—Since when are we putting a label on this?

His smile takes on a strained quality—Just go with it.

I guess he meant it when he said that he might use this opportunity to bring up the fake engagement. All at once I feel caught between two worlds—like a statue on display that's expected to somehow talk and engage and react too.

"Nice to meet you," Greyson says, shaking my hand.

He's got the same killer jawline as Nolan, although his dark hair is curlier and much shorter, while his eyes are two icy blue shards, that soften when they land on Harley.

"Hope you like spaghetti," Harley says, already sauntering into the kitchen, her blonde shoulder-length braids bobbing with each step. "Because that's what we're having. Although I might have some leftover casserole I could heat up..."

"Spaghetti sounds great," I say.

Inside, the also plant-filled kitchen leads onto a monstera-bordered dining area, where a long table has some people already sitting at it.

"That sad chap there at the end, that's my brother Emerson," Nolan says, gesturing to a handsome blond man with, sure enough, sad blue eyes.

"Thanks," Emerson says, deadpan, although he smiles politely at me.

As we shake hands, Nolan adds, "This man here is all set to be America's next top piano player. Don't sulk at me like that, brother, I brought you a gift."

He takes an old-looking pamphlet out of his bag that brightens Emerson's face. "How'd you find this?"

Nolan draws himself up importantly. "I have my connections." He grins. "OK, OK, it was eBay. Who knew some old piano knickknack could be so expensive."

"Some old piano knickknack," Emerson sputters, although he's still smiling as he gives what I can now see is a music booklet a little wave. "This is Mozart's 35th symphony, printed over 200 years ago!"

"Yeah, yeah, I just saw it was old and piano-y, so I figured you'd be into it," Nolan says with a dismissive wave, already taking something else out of his bag. "Now, for the host and hostess..."

"You didn't!" Harley exclaims, accepting the orange-colored bottle with a grin.

"You didn't," Greyson says, with much less enthusiasm.

"It wasn't easy finding it, let me tell you," Nolan declares with a grin. "I didn't even know orange wine was a thing until you told me about it."

"It's great—we'll have it tonight," Harley says, rushing over to the stovetop to check on the spaghetti. "You'll see."

Now, Nolan turns to the man I've been shyly eyeing for the past minute or so. The one who is, unmistakably, his twin.

"You made it," Nolan says, throwing his arms around him.

While they're still hugging, he twists my way and, jerking his head towards his brother, says, "This is Landon. My twin. Some would even say my better half."

"I didn't notice," I say.

They crack up and the dark-haired woman still sitting, says, "I like her."

"Then you have good taste," Nolan says as they draw apart. He gestures to her. "Sierra, meet Kyra."

Kyra is short, dark-haired and pretty, and has a strong, firm handshake.

"Never screw Kyra over," Nolan stage whispers, letting his eyebrows jump significantly. "She's a lawyer. A damn good one."

Kyra laughs good-humoredly. "You flatter me."

Landon's hand goes to the small of her back. "No—you're the best in New York."

It really is a bit galling how alike they look, Landon and Nolan. Same strong jawline, same light-colored straight hair, same hazel eyes.

"Spaghetti's ready!" Harley announces with a flourish of the ladle.

"Already?" Nolan says, although he's grinning. "But we just got here."

"Shut up and eat my food," Harley says, aiming the ladle at him like a sword.

We all laugh.

CHAPTER 17

Nolan

"She seems to be getting along well with everyone," Landon says quietly after dinner.

All three women are in the den on the couches, cackling with their heads bent over our baby pictures, while Emerson and Greyson do the dishes.

The ladies can't get over how fat Landon and I were as toddlers, how solemn Greyson was. And Emerson's propensity for smearing his food all over his forehead has always been a crowd favorite.

"Of course," I say in a faux-offended tone. "I only bring quality women into the Storm household."

"All jokes aside," he says, a bit quieter now. "You seem happy."

I snort. "I've always been the happiest one in this family. The one with the best sense of humor, too."

He snorts. "And so humble."

"She does seem to get along with everyone," I remark, frowning. I can't seem to stop my gaze from sneaking over to the den to check on her protectively. "Not that I expected any different."

"Looks like you might actually be settling down, brother," Landon jokes.

"Let's not get ahead of ourselves," I grumble.

His easy smile falls. "Why bring her here, then?"

"I can't have my own reasons for doing things? Damn it, why do you all have to micro-analyze every other thing I do?"

I scowl at how much of a defensive idiot I sound. But hell, I was having fun here with Sierra, and then Landon has to make his comments and ruin it.

That's what I like about being with Sierra. Everything seems easy, to not require much thought. It just works.

"Forget it," I say. "I'm just nervy."

"Clearly," Landon says.

"How's Emerson, anyway?" I ask.

"He's seemed to enjoy staying with us the past few nights," Landon says. "He and Madison actually get along pretty great. Those two can play Star Wars Monopoly for hours."

"Great, but he knows that he can stay with me for however long he needs, right?" I add.

Landon's eyebrows flatten in the way that I know means he's hesitant. "I'm not sure that's the best place for him right now."

"What's that supposed to mean?"

"You and Jax are big partiers," Landon says flatly. "Whether it's at clubs or house parties, you guys go hard. You really think that's the best thing for Emerson to be around right now?"

"I did say that I'd slow down," I growl, although he has a point.

I head for the bathroom without another word.

It shouldn't matter, Landon as much as saying that I'm a bad influence, but it does. Lately, things have been confusing—with the business, Sierra, basically everything.

Normally, I'd just laugh off what he said, but now... Emerson almost died the other night. Jesus.

As I head back, I linger outside the main room and listen to the happy chatter inside. Sounds like my brothers have joined the girls, and they're all chuckling at the photos of us as kids, how Mom liked to dress us up in these crazy matching retro raincoats and bathrobes. I can hear Sierra's voice in there, as delighted and at ease as the others.

She really fits in.

Part of me wants to keep on standing here, or even just walk away. So I don't have to do what I came here to do.

I still could.

I could turn around and walk out that door. I could keep on seeing Sierra how we have been, keep things how they are.

But I already ran the idea by her. There's not much other choice at this point.

Sure, I can pay her out of pocket, even finance the renos like that too. But there's only so much cash I have in my savings account. It won't cover paying her and all the renos, and then where will I be?

Besides, this fake engagement doesn't have to change anything.

Walking inside the room, I feel like if I even glimpsed my reflection right now, I'd punch it. I can't look at Sierra as I say the words: "There's something we have to tell you."

It feels like I'm reading off a script someone else prepared.

I don't even wait for everyone to quiet down before I say: "Sierra and I, we're engaged."

CHAPTER 18

Sierra

"Well, that didn't go quite so bad," Nolan says cheerfully as he drives me home.

I don't even try to answer.

If his version of 'not quite so bad' involves everyone going speechless with shock and Nolan hustling me out of there like I have contagious leprosy, then sure, I guess it didn't.

Sitting in his car, all I want is a blanket to wrap myself in. And bury my head in, maybe even cry into.

I'm being melodramatic, probably, but the way Nolan just blurted it out—we're engaged—seemed so out of left field.

Yes, Nolan as much as said that he'd bring it up.

And yes, even arriving at the dinner, I partially expected him to announce it.

Only, practically as soon as I set foot into the plant-filled, activity-bustling house, I clean forgot about it. Everyone seemed so easy to talk to and happy, hell, Nolan seemed so happy, that I guess I really bought it. That Nolan brought me there because I was his girlfriend, who he liked.

Just for that reason.

Now, I just don't know.

"How did Emerson look to you?" Nolan asks lightly.

"A little sad at the beginning, but overall fine. Why?"

"No reason," he says, just as lightly.

"OK."

If Nolan wants to play this game of feelings tag, where it seems I'm chasing him until he decides to stand still, then he's free to. I'm done getting myself hurt.

"Earlier this week, he just…" Nolan frowns, tendons showing on his hands as he clenches the steering wheel hard. "He got hospitalized for drinking too much. He's going through stuff with this latest breakup of his."

"Oh, I had no idea," I say. "I'm so sorry."

"I am too." The tense tan of his skin looks like a mask, his eyes hollow stones. "I'm supposed to be his big brother, to look out for him, and instead I'm just…"

He gives his head a swift shake, as if to physically throw off the thought.

"Anyway." He glances at me. "You had a good time?"

"Yeah," I say.

If he's not going to bring up the elephant in the room—how his announcement of our engagement was the buzzkill of the night—then I'm not going to.

"Good," he says.

"Good," I say.

And though he looks like he wants to say more, he doesn't.

Once I get home, there's no more doubt in my mind about this Nolan Storm article job.

After all, he seems fine enough with using me to suit his fake engagement. Why should I have qualms over writing some stupid article about him?

So, I sit down to my laptop and start typing: The first thing you need to know about Nolan Storm is that he isn't what he seems.

The next few weeks go by in a blur. I get more done on the article and even send a rough draft Maurice's way. In return, he sends some of the money my way.

I get more articles done for Nolan, who's over the moon about them.

We don't visit his family again. I don't let him visit mine.

He takes me out every few nights, but it's not the same.

We go through the motions: make conversation, laugh and have fun on the dates, even sleep together. And yet, the next morning, all I'm left with is an unmistakable feeling of emptiness.

Like I just ate a bunch of cotton candy for a meal. Like I still need some nourishment.

It's probably because the fake engagement is still hanging over our heads.

Nolan hasn't mentioned it, almost seems afraid to. But the less he says about it, the more it seems to grow. Even the twins have stopped teasing me about it.

I realize as time goes on that I feel guilty too.

No matter what a jerk Nolan has been to me, that still doesn't make me writing a secret article about him right.

In the end, it's a conversation over the phone with Maurice that decides it for me.

"Hate to be a downer," he grumbles, in a tone that sounds like it doesn't hate anything except maybe life itself, "but you got anything else to put in that article of yours that isn't going to make me yawn?"

"What did you have in mind?" I say, careful to keep the annoyance out of my voice.

After all, this man is my boss.

"Something spicy, controversial." For the first time in our conversations, Maurice actually sounds excited. "Something to make everyone infuriated or shocked."

"Come on," he insists when I try suggesting something else that is apparently yawn-worthy. "You working so closely with Nolan like this—you must have some good private juice on him. Something that will shock people out of their socks."

"Not really," I say quietly.

Of course, I have more than enough 'private' material to put in the article, if I really wanted to. But no way would I betray Nolan like that.

"Big shot like that," Maurice insists. "He must've been a jerk to someone, done something horrible."

"Why are you so sure it would be something horrible?" I ask.

"Just—instinct," he says in an odd tone. "These big-shot guys, they're all the same. Besides, Nolan Storm, he's a tool, he—"

"Are you wanting me to write an article about him, or an article bashing him?" I say, cutting to the chase. "Because it's really starting to feel like the latter."

"It's just an angle," Maurice protests. "I have to sell this thing, you know. If nobody cares, I can't sell it."

"So, if I were to mention how he wants to build an educational center to help military and ex-military people, then—"

"Bo-ring," he interrupts. "Now, if you had evidence that he was collecting money for this center, then spending it on his gambling addiction, then we might have something."

I pause.

Part of me has been avoiding this conversation instinctively, I realize. Ever since Maurice and I first met in that cat cafe.

"I'm not going to take that angle," I say quietly. "I'm sorry."

"It's not an angle." Now Maurice sounds downright livid. "It's the truth. Nolan Storm is a scheming, lying asshole who takes what he wants when he wants with no concern for consequences, let alone anyone else."

If I were holding something, I'm pretty sure I would've just dropped it. "What?"

"You heard me"—he's all but snarling, now—"if you can't find any dirt on him, then you're lying."

"I'm sorry," I say firmly. "But I won't do the kind of article you're asking me for right now. And that's final."

"So, what—you take my money and run, is that it?" he sneers.

"No. You've paid me a quarter of the agreed-upon price. You can have the work I completed for that, and we'll call it even."

"A bunch of unusable shit, great."

"Hey," I snap. "If you wanted this type of article, then you should've mentioned it up front. You have no one to blame but yourself."

His response is the beep of him hanging up.

I stand there in my kitchen for a few seconds.

Horatio trots along the floor, his too-long nails clacking on the linoleum. I make a mental note to give them a chop.

I sit down on a kitchen chair, exhaling a breath that I didn't realize I was holding in.

There.

It's done.

Despite the fact that I basically just lost $8,000, it feels like a weight has been lifted off my shoulders. For the past few weeks, I've known this wasn't right.

Even if Nolan was an ass about the fake engagement, that still doesn't make this right.

Later that day, after cutting Horatio's nails, I stop by Mom's to help her pick out a place to move into for the next few months. I'm met with a shitty surprise when her robin's egg-blue door opens.

"Oh." Peyton's forehead creases. "It's you."

"Great to see you too," I chime in, striding in past her before my hatred of her overrules all else. Yes, Mom didn't mention that she'd be here, and yes, it was probably deliberate, but right now, the most important thing is making sure that Mom finds a nice new place. "Let's just get through today, for Mom."

"That's what I was going to say," she says prissily, just as Mom sweeps into the room.

"Isn't this nice!" she declares. "All of us here together."

Despite Mom's determined smile, I can see that she's on edge. She's wearing her big pale pink angora sweater, her self-proclaimed 'comfort sweater'.

Underneath the mandarin air freshener, there's still a hint of smoke smell here in the house.

"First, we're getting fuel," Peyton proclaims, already heading out the door with her hot pink heels clacking across the wood floor.

Guess that answers the question of who's going to be in charge today. Not that I had any doubt as soon as I saw my dear big sister.

I turn to Mom, trying not sigh.

"Don't," she says tersely, hitching her patent black purse up her shoulder. "I just need both my daughters here with me today.

"Yes, Mom," I say dutifully, with a nod. "Anything you need."

"Well." Mom heads to the car, with a small smile. "Peyton might be right. Some coffee would be nice."

We get to Dunkin' Donuts a few minutes later. Once we walk in through the door, I'm in for another surprise.

"You," I say, coming to a stop when I see who's leaving.

Nolan stops, looking as surprised as I probably do, holding his bag of donuts as if he's just been caught committing a crime. "You?"

All of a sudden, Peyton gets all fluttery and grin-y, the way she gets around any attractive man. Forget that she has a fiance. "Who's this?"

"This is Nolan, my..." I shoot Nolan a warning glare—Bring up the fake engagement, and you'll live to regret it.

"We're dating," Nolan says, with a smile at my mom just as he sticks out his hand. "I'm Nolan Storm. It's a pleasure to finally meet you."

Good save.

"Really?" Peyton says, looking him up and down.

She says it in the tone she'd use if I suddenly told her that, yes, I can leap tall buildings in a single bound.

Clearly, she thinks Nolan is way, way, way too good for me.

Mom, however, beams. "Sierra hinted that she might be seeing someone, but it's great to finally put a name and face to it. And... Nolan Storm... hmm, now, why does that name seem so familiar?"

"Hold on." Now Peyton's heavily mascara-ed blue eyes look ready to pop out of her head. I'm almost enjoying this. "You're not... part of the Storm family?"

Nolan just chuckles. "One of the less interesting brothers, but yes, that's us. I actually met Sierra at my comedy club restaurant."

Peyton's jaw has dropped and can't seem to find its way back.

"Anyway," I say, taking a step towards the counter. "We're just here to grab a coffee before checking out some places for my mom. Boring stuff."

"Doesn't sound boring to me," Nolan says with a charming smile.

Is he getting at what I think he is?

"Of course, you're welcome to join," Mom says easily. "Although you probably already have plans?"

Nolan shakes his head. "Joining would be great. If Sierra's OK with it?"

I resist the urge to glare at him, instead saying, "Of course. Why wouldn't I be?"

As if I hadn't been basically forced into this by the pair of them.

"I'll pick up the coffees, then," Nolan says, adding with a wave of his Dunkin' Donuts punch card, before anyone can protest, "I'm two away from getting a free one anyway. My friend loves this place."

"I'll join you to make sure you order the right kinds," I say with a forced cheeriness. "Mom and Peyton, you just stay here, I know what you like."

At the counter, waiting in line, I hiss, "What are you doing?"

Nolan sips his coffee with an annoyingly innocent expression. "I thought I could get to know your family. Is that so wrong?"

"Yes," I say tersely.

He frowns. "You met mine. I figured it was only fair."

"You only had me meet yours so you could announce our fake engagement to them," I point out.

His scowl deepens, spreading to his eyes. "That was only part of it. Anyway—you want me to make an excuse and go now? I can do that."

"No," I say with a sigh. "It's too late now. If you leave after we talk like this, it'll be too convenient. I won't hear the end of it from Mom or Peyton all day."

"Glad you're so thrilled for me to be meeting your family," Nolan says, deadpan.

My response is just to glare at him some more, since by now, it's our turn at the counter.

I tell the cashier our orders, Nolan pays, and we head back to Mom and Peyton.

"Thank you," Mom tells him, smiling as though she just won the lottery. "Sierra really found a good one in you, Nolan."

Nolan chuckles. "I hope to live up to that, Ms...."

"Oh, call me Donna," she says, chuckling herself.

"We should go," I say. "Or we're going to miss some of the viewings."

"This one's a regular old buzzkill," Peyton says to Nolan, gesturing to me with a little laugh. "I'm surprised a comedian would be drawn to that."

Nolan just winks. "Opposites attract."

Peyton cackles, way louder than necessary.

"In all seriousness, though," Nolan says. "Sierra is fun to be around. I'm the one who feels lucky to be around her."

He frowns a little after saying it, as if he hadn't intended for it to slip out.

"Right, well, while you're all talking about me, I'll be in the car," I say, striding off.

Really, I just want some air. And space to think.

Maybe I'm freaking out, but too freaking bad.

What the hell is Nolan doing? Is this all just part of his fake engagement plan? If so, why hasn't he mentioned it yet?

Maybe I should try acting more normal and happy around him, but I can't help but be suspicious.

The last time I let my guard down around Nolan, he impromptu announced that we were engaged in front of his whole family. How do I know he won't do that this time with mine?

In the car, the 'fun' continues. Mom, Peyton and Nolan chat as easily as if they were old friends. Nolan tells them about a few of our dates and seeing the Peppers.

"I can't believe I've been so out of the loop," Mom says, shooting me a scolding look. "Sierra, when were you planning on telling me all this?"

How about when I knew whether Nolan and me were the real deal and could say for certain that he wasn't just using me as part of some elaborate fake engagement plot?

"Don't be so hard on her," Nolan says. "Sierra's just being cautious. I can respect that."

"That's understandable," Mom agrees. "But when were you planning on having us meet, Sierra?"

How about when I knew whether Nolan and me were the real deal and could say for certain that he wasn't using me as part of some elaborate fake engagement plot?

"You're right, Mom," I say instead. "Sorry. I just got caught up with all the work lately and didn't plan out a good time."

Nolan, to his credit, doesn't mention that he's already tried meeting my family a few times before. I guess I'm not completely furious at him.

"Speaking of which," Mom says, "how's that article been going? The independent one from that man?"

I gulp.

Way to bring up the last thing I'd want you to, Mom.

"You've got another job going on?" Nolan says, turning to me with what looks like genuine interest.

"Yeah, I just quit, though," I say. "Didn't like my boss."

"Oh." Mom tries to keep the disappointment out of her voice. "I thought you said the pay was extremely good?"

"It was," I say quickly. "Just not the right fit."

"I'm sure she had her reasons," Peyton cuts in, in a tone that suggests they were stupid ones.

I guess me praying that she'll focus on driving is pretty much hopeless.

"Anyway," I say, as she parks the car, "looks like we're here!"

The rest of the day goes better.

Nolan charms Mom and Peyton enough that Peyton hardly has time to try pissing me off. Nolan even talks to some of the landlords on Mom's behalf. At one place, he manages to halve the price. At another, he straight-up tells Mom to turn it down.

"I know the contractor who made this building," he explains as we leave. "The man cuts corners in everything. You'd have plumbing and electrical problems from day one. Not worth it."

By the end, Mom's decided on a nice two-bedroom in town, and Nolan has bargained the price down for her.

"Nolan Storm," Peyton says, stepping forward and touching him on the chest once we're finished. "I do think that you're our knight in shining armor.

Frowning in confusion, Nolan steps back. "Thanks. But it wasn't really a big deal."

"Well, you'll have to let me take you out sometime to make up for it," she declares.

I just gape at her.

I have to give it to her: Peyton has balls.

I mean, I've never seen her as Pollyanna, or anything but a selfish bitch, but this takes the cake: Flirting this blatantly with my boyfriend while literally right in front of me.

"If Sierra's there, I will be too," Nolan says stoutly, nodding to me.

I could kiss him right now.

"But right now," he continues, "I'm afraid I do have plans... with Sierra—if she's free?"

I find myself grinning. "Oh, I'm free."

Anything to get away from my evil sister.

And after today, I actually want to spend some more time with Nolan. He made what was slated to be an agonizing afternoon actually bearable.

"It's a surprise, though," he says, with a wink.

Mom grins at us. "You two have fun. Thanks for helping me out, both of you. Lovely to meet you, Nolan."

"My pleasure," Nolan says, smiling.

Peyton is squinting at Nolan as if he's a sign she can't read. "So, you're actually going off... with her?"

"They are dating, Peyton," Mom says with a small laugh. Knowing her, she's once again reinterpreted Peyton's inborn bitchiness as 'a bit of confusion'. "Now, you two have fun!"

"I can't think of anyone I'd rather spend tonight with," Nolan says, kissing me on the cheek.

Then, he takes my hand and we're off.

"Whew," I say, as soon as he's driven off.

"Your sister..." he begins hesitantly.

"Hates my guts," I finish for him.

"Ah," he says. "I wondered."

"Thank you," I tell him. "At first, I didn't think you coming was a good idea, but I actually had a great time. I really appreciate all the advice and help you gave to my mom."

"It was good meeting your family," Nolan says. "Although there is something I'd like from you."

My heart drops.

Great.

So much for him doing this just for the sake of it.

There's a price—of course there's a price. I should've known.

CHAPTER 19

Nolan

The car stopped at a red light, I glance over to scan her face.

She's gorgeous, of course, even with her red-brown hair pulled back in a messy ponytail and little makeup. But she looks tense. Not like someone who's about to give me anything.

"Stay the night with me," I say, grinning.

Sierra's eyes semi-squint. "That's it?"

"What do you mean, that's it?"

"That's all you want?" She sounds surprised.

"Why is that so hard to believe?"

She lets out a little laugh, which ends in an easing of her features and body. "I don't know. Because of how you said it? Who says 'although there is something I'd like from you' when they just want you to stay the night?"

I chuckle. "Me?"

She laughs. "Clearly."

Damn, I want to kiss her right here and now. Take her right here and now. Make her mine right here and now.

But for now, I have to keep driving. Get us where we're going.

"I guess I asked it like that, since it's not just a sleepover at my place," I admit. "Or at a hotel."

"Now I am intrigued."

"It's this cabin," I explain. "Landon and Kyra went there years and years ago for Valentine's Day. They loved it. I thought maybe, if you wanted—"

"Yes."

"That easy?"

Her nose crinkles as her expression grows wary. "Why, is it rotting and filled with mold?"

"No." I frown at her. "I booked it for tonight. It's an Airbnb. Has a Jacuzzi, some hammocks outside and everything. Plus any toiletries we might need."

"Then yes, of course yes."

I grin at her. She grins back.

"Good," I say.

"Good," she says.

And half an hour later, we're there. It doesn't take us long to drop off our things and get settled.

Sierra does a quick tour of the place before coming back to embrace me.

I chuckle. "It's that good?"

"It's that good."

She isn't wrong. The wooden walls and rustic furniture are beautiful, and the view of pine trees outside doesn't hurt.

Afterwards, we go to a little Italian restaurant in town that has some delicious meatballs and chocolate lava cake. Then, it's back to the cabin for us.

By now, it's nighttime.

"I'm thinking it's time for this, and this," I say, taking out two bottles.

Sierra goggles at one. "What kind of wine is that?"

I bust out laughing. "The bubble bath kind?"

Laughing, Sierra surveys the bottle of bubble bath. "How was I supposed to guess? The way you brought them out together…"

I make a face. God is she cute sometimes. "If you really want, we can try drinking the bubble bath and bathing in the wine, but…"

She gives me a playful slap. "I take it back, you goon."

I smirk. "Goon, now that's a new one."

"Just kiss me, you jerk."

"Gladly."

Next second, our lips are sweeping together, and I realize what today has been missing: this.

Her sweet scent filling my nostrils. Her soft lips moving with mine. Our fingers entwining and clasping.

I finally pull away with difficulty. "Bubble bath first, or we'll never get to it."

"Agreed," Sierra says, catching her breath.

The hot water comes fast enough and feels damn good. Before I know it, we're in the expansive pale pink porcelain hot tub, surrounded by bubbles.

"What are you doing?" Sierra asks as I swish some away with my hands, peering under the water.

"Trying to see," I say.

Realizing what I mean, she splashes me. "Perv!"

"What?" I protest. "I can't enjoy a work of art like my girlfriend's body?"

"Your fake fiancee's," she shoots back.

Suddenly, the air goes out of the room.

I have the ridiculous urge to take what she said and physically toss it out of here.

"Forget it," she says softly.

"Gladly," I say, taking her in my arms.

I almost say it: Forget it.

Although I'd mean something completely different—something I'm starting to think we both want to forget about.

Only, I already tried once, and it's better just to not think about it. Avoid it.

My hands move over her body under the vanilla-bubbled hot water, and pleased murmurs come out of Sierra.

Goddamn does she feel good: her hips, her breasts. I could touch her like this forever. I'm getting hard already.

When we finally do kiss again, I can't help myself. 'Slow' doesn't exist. Only she exists. Her lips, her moans, her body.

I sit her on top of me and, under the water, my fingers slip inside of her. Her neck arches and she groans even louder.

"That's it," I growl, flickering my fingers into her faster. "Moan for me, baby."

And does she ever. She moans until her back is arched too, until she's shaking, coming. I hold her the whole time.

When our lips meet again, I can't wait any longer. My arms wrap around her and I thrust myself inside of her. We both groan at the same time.

She's so wet. So tight. So perfect for me.

I could fuck Sierra Hill forever.

Our pelvises slap together as our bodies strain for more. More pleasure. More in and out. More deeper.

The water sloshing over the sides of the tub with the frantic movement of our bodies doesn't distract us.

I fuck her into the side of the tub, and her pussy clasps eagerly back on my cock. We move easily from one position to another. I can't get over how hot Sierra looks with her face strained yet slack with pleasure.

I could take a picture of that face and hang it on my wall.

But it's happening too fast. I don't usually get this excited this fast. It takes all I have to hold it in as Sierra loses it once, then again, riding the ecstatic waves of her climax. Only once she's coming for the third time, more powerfully than ever, do I let myself lose it too.

Fuck, it feels so good... so right...

Afterwards, we lie there and let the hot water beat against our bodies. I turn on the bubbles with the switch on the side of the hot tub.

"Double bubble action," I quip, and we laugh as the tub splashes even more bubbles to join our vanilla ones.

I don't tell her this, because it's a little fucking ridiculous and pointless, but Sierra looks more beautiful than ever right now. Her hair slicked back, her eyes happier than I've ever seen them.

I want her looking like this more. I want to see this face every day of my life.

I give my head an abrupt shake.

What the actual fuck is going on with me lately?

Must be the wine. Only... we haven't had any yet.

Who fucking knows.

"Know what I'm thinking?" I murmur in Sierra's ear.

"That was some good sex?" she suggests.

We both crack up at that. "Yes," I say. "But no. I was thinking that it might be time for some stargazing."

"But the tub," Sierra protests with a sigh, nuzzling closer up to me with a pout. "So comfy. So warm."

"There's some cozy bathrobes," I point out, gesturing to the ones hanging on the back of the bathroom door.

Sierra eyes the fluffy white things warily.

"Here," I say, picking her up. "Let me help you."

"Nolan!" she protests, giggling and wriggling to no avail.

"Come on," I coax her, placing her on her feet and starting to help her into a robe. "You'll thank me later."

"Hruh," is all she says as she reluctantly lets me help her into the robe.

A few minutes later, we're outside in the two-person hammock, gazing up at the stars.

"Thank you," she whispers. "Holy crap."

"Holy crap is right," is all I say.

Sure, there's words for what we're seeing. But they wouldn't do it justice, this astral symphony filling the sky before us. Star after star after star after star. More than I ever thought existed in my wildest dreams.

"It makes you wonder," I say quietly. "How this is all up there all along, only we can't see it in the city."

Makes you wonder what else is there right in front of your nose that you're refusing to see, either because of your current situation, or something else.

She nestles closer up to me.

"I mean it," she says quietly. "This is amazing. Thank you. You keep surprising me."

Her voice warms me from the inside out. It's an odd feeling.

"Good," I say.

"Good," she says.

"Good," I say.

She just laughs. "That's it?"

"It's a good word," I protest. "Good?"

She laughs again. "Good."

"I, just…" She goes quiet. Bathed in moonlight, her contemplative face is absurdly beautiful. "We never went camping when I was little. My mom was against it, since my dad loved it so much. Said it would just remind her too much of him, just hurt too much."

"Doesn't sound like he was a great guy," I say.

"He wasn't." Her contemplative expression goes sad. "I don't know how he could live with himself, just walking away from his own children, but he found a way to do it. Anyway, I'm lucky. I have a good mom who was always there for me. Not everyone can say that."

"No." Suddenly I feel heavy, like the hammock could snap under my weight. "Not everyone can."

And suddenly, I don't know why, I'm saying, "My mom walked off."

"Oh."

She doesn't ask me to say more, to explain it, but I do. I don't know why, but I want to.

"She didn't give hardly any notice to any of us, either. I guess she was just fed up with my dad and all that, once she found out about his cheating. But she just walked out of our lives. We were close—at least I thought we were—I lived with her for months after the full extent of the cheating was revealed. But one day, she just wasn't there anymore. First, she claimed an impromptu vacation to Barbados. Then she said she wasn't coming back. Finally she stopped calling altogether. I guess it just hurt too much."

"She just abandoned you?" Sierra asks, turning on her stomach to eye me with sad shock.

I shrug. "Not much different from what your dad did."

"I don't know." She frowns. "What he did was horrible, sure, but we were too little to really realize what had happened. You were how old?"

"A teen," I admit. "And yeah. It took me a long time to get over it. I'm not sure I have, even now."

Her hand finds mine, squeezes it.

It doesn't make sense—it shouldn't make it better—but it does.

"I'm sorry," she says.

"I am too," I say. "Just—for her, my dad was the love of her life. High school sweethearts and all that. To have to stick around and live with his betrayals... I guess she just figured it was easier moving away and starting a new life. My Dad tried finding her after, but he never did manage it."

"But to just abandon her children," Sierra says softly.

"She calls now, every so often," I say. "I think once a year with the others. I don't keep in touch with her, though."

"I don't blame you," Sierra says.

We lie there for a while longer.

She feels so good in my arms, so warm.

"Sierra?" I say.

"Yeah?" she says.

I almost say it. Tell her how I've never talked about my mom to any girl, never taken any girl here.

How, even though I heard about this place years and years ago, I've never known any woman I wanted to take here—until now.

But instead, I just hold her closer and say, "Goodnight."

"Goodnight," she murmurs.

And because she's here, I know it'll be so.

CHAPTER 20

Sierra

"Rise and shine, beautiful," Nolan says.

I pause.

I feel lovely, cozy. Warm.

I can hear some robins singing. I can feel a shaft of morning light warming me.

The last thing I want to do is break this beautiful dream.

But when his fingers burrow into my armpit, my eyes snap open as I squeal. "Nolan!"

He just laughs, tickling me furiously, before rushing away with an irreverent grin. "Breakfast's ready!"

"Ugh, you!" I groan.

"I can eat yours?" he offers, leaning against the side of the cabin with a jaunty smile.

If I had anything to throw at him, I would. As it stands, I just get up and head into the cabin with a determined glare. "This better be good."

"You're not much of a morning person, are you?" he jokes.

"Because it's completely normal to love being woken up via tickling," I shoot back.

Although my frown can't stay when I see the feast Nolan's prepared us: glistening fried eggs, crunchy home fries, crispy bacon and grilled tomato.

"I can think of worse ways to be woken up," Nolan argues.

"Deadly spider bite," I agree.

He grins, his eyebrows jumping. "A piano falling on you."

"Being pushed off a building."

"An alarm set five minutes after your final exam ended."

We both chuckle as we sit down.

"I mean it, though." Nolan's expression goes faux-concerned as he reaches over to my plate with his fork. "If you're still too sleepy to eat…"

I elbow his arm away and dig in. "Screw you."

He's still all smiles. "Gladly."

We enjoy our breakfast, then Nolan pounces on me and we make love one more time. And then one more time.

And then… just once more.

When the 'last time' we promised each other actually is the last time, I can hardly walk. Him going down on me is nothing short of incredible.

"So, I was thinking," he says as we drive away, smiling like goofy fools. "If you're free today, we could have the day to ourselves."

"Sounds good," I say.

But when I check my phone a few minutes later, I groan.

"What?" Nolan asks.

"I forgot, I'm supposed to meet the twins today for a late lunch."

"Ah." He eyes me. "Well, I'm not going to invite myself into your plans for a second time, but…"

I smirk at him. "Fine."

"Yeah?" He brightens.

"Yeah," I say. "They've heard enough about you. It's about time you all meet."

He makes a faux horrified face. "Should I be worried?"

I raise my eyebrows. "I don't know, should you?"

"Absolutely not." Nolan draws himself up with an upward flick of her chin. "A stellar man like myself, I have nothing to worry about."

I snort.

"Besides," he continues. "You told me that they too are twins. All twins worldwide have an inborn kinship. You will see."

I just laugh.

We stop by both our places so we can get changed and I can walk Horatio. By the time we make it to the diner, we're five minutes late.

"You're late," Wynona declares, her navy-blue lipstick lips frowning as she views me, then, when she sees Nolan, "Oh."

"Ohhhhhhh." Josie says, her neon pink lips drawing into a smile. "It's him."

"It is I," Nolan agrees pleasantly, throwing out a hand. "A fellow twin."

Josie snorts, shaking it. "I like him."

"It's a bit early for that," Wynona comments drily.

"Like you and Mr. Lumberjack talking wedding plans?" Josie shoots back innocently.

Wynona cheeks redden. "We were wasted and it wasn't serious. And his name is Wyatt, as I've told you before."

"My, I have been out of the loop," I say, grinning at Wynona.

Her scowl gets fiercer as she unconsciously balls up a napkin in her hand. "Enough about me. We're here finally meeting your Nolan."

"I like to think of myself as an independent agent," Nolan remarks placidly.

We all just chuckle.

"So, Sierra isn't your girlfriend?" Josie says, cocking her blonde pigtailed head.

Her tone doesn't indicate this is a test, but I can tell from her tell-me-more body language that it is. Josie has uncovered many men's red flags in this seemingly innocent way.

"She is," Nolan says without any hesitation. "We just came back from a cabin getaway in the woods, in fact."

"Aw!" Josie says.

"It was pretty amazing," I admit, as he and I finally sit down in the booth. "There was this amazing bubble bath—and the stars…"

"I'm ordering pancakes," Wynona announces.

"Don't mind her," Josie tells Nolan, throwing a dismissive wave at Wynona. "She's just judgmental, and you didn't make the greatest first impression, so…"

Nolan nods. "Understatement: I made the worst first impression. I was a complete dick."

Finally, Wynona smiles, with a pleased nod of her own. "Ah, so you are self-aware."

Nolan winces. "I guess I deserved that."

"Can we just order food and save the grilling for later?" I ask.

"Fine," Josie says, pouting at me before turning a stern frown at Nolan. "Though I'll have you know I do have questions that need to be answered."

Nolan manages to chuckle. "What have I gotten myself into?"

"Nothing a good guy wouldn't get through," Wynona says mildly.

I resist the urge to sigh. Maybe us coming here today wasn't such a great idea.

I was just riding such a high from last night that I didn't really think it through.

Although once we finally do order—blueberry pancakes for all—it doesn't go completely horrible.

"So," Josie says, steepling her pink-and-purple-nailed hands as she regards Nolan with a severe look. "What are your intentions with our Sierra?"

Nolan's hand sweeps to his chest. "Completely honorable, I do swear!"

We all giggle, and he continues, "In all seriousness, I really like her."

"We know about the fake engagement," Wynona cuts in.

"Ah," Nolan says, shooting me a sidelong look. "I'm not sure that I'm wanting to go through with that after all."

My heart leaps, although I keep my mouth shut.

"Not sure," Wynona continues in a dangerous tone. "Or just don't want to deal with her crazy twin friends bitching at you?"

"Why can't it be both?" Nolan asks.

Josie giggles, Wynona glares.

"Can Sierra and I talk this over later today?" he asks.

"Of course," Josie says. "Although I'm sure you can understand why we can't totally be on Team Nolan, with what we know."

Nolan nods. "That's fair." He eyes them. "Is it my turn for questions now?"

Josie says "Yes" at the same time that Wynona says "No."

Nolan leans over the table with a devilish smile anyway. "What is Sierra's deepest, darkest secret that she wouldn't want me to know?"

"What kind of crap friends do you think we are?" Josie demands.

"That her dog Horatio shits on rugs, especially nice ones," Wynona says smoothly.

We all crack up at that.

"It's not his fault," I say. "He's a rescue."

Josie shudders. "Anyone who spends more than a month in the company of your sister needs to be rescued."

"She was a horrible dog owner," I explain to Nolan. "And this isn't just my dislike of her speaking. She sometimes wouldn't take him for walks for days on end—just used these pee pads that she'd get her maid to clean up... it was bad."

"Your sister doesn't sound like the greatest person," Nolan comments diplomatically.

"You think?" Josie says. "She made me cry on my birthday when I was twelve."

"She forced me to lock myself in a locker and not come out until school was over in ninth grade," Wynona recounts.

"Jesus," Nolan says. "This woman sounds like the Antichrist."

"That about sums it," I say, all of us chuckling.

Once our meals are delivered, we gobble them down. Then, it's some more easy chitchat with the twins before it's time for us to go. Nolan insists on paying the bill.

"Is this your way of bribing yourself into our good graces?" Wynona point-blank asks him.

Nolan just smiles. "Is it working?"

"Now that you mention it," I say, smiling my own evil smile, "there is this new pink Volkswagen beetle Josie was eyeing..."

We separate, laughing.

Being with Nolan is like going around places with a chocolate in your mouth. Like wherever we go, whatever we do, it'll be good because he's here.

The rest of the day, we run errands that would normally be mundane—but aren't because he's here. We go grocery shopping and buy weird fruit. We get enamored with some bland cookies with a funny baby on the front called Parle-G. We try on crazy scarves and ridiculous hats at Macy's until I've laughed so much at our reflections that my mouth hurts.

By the end of the day, back at my place, I'm so exhausted that I have to drag myself off the couch to walk Horatio. Nolan and I making love three times probably didn't help, either.

That night, as I'm half-asleep in Nolan's arms, he murmurs, "I really like you."

I pause—does he know I'm awake?

His big hand runs over my hair affectionately, and it hits me then: no, he doesn't think so.

"But it's a secret," he says, chuckling to myself. "So, don't tell."

I won't, I think to myself, as I drift off, happier than ever. Promise.

CHAPTER 21

Nolan

Goddamn is it a good morning.

I've got my girl in my arms, it's a long weekend, and I feel damn good.

The past day was a happy blur. Even if I didn't totally win over her friends, it's only a matter of time.

They brought up a good point, too. The more I think about it, the more I'm starting to realize that this fake engagement is more trouble than it's worth.

Screw the money. Screw my dad's will.

What's it worth if I lose my girl, the only thing that's really mattered to me for a long time now?

In the bathroom, on the toilet, I check my phone.

You need to see this, Landon's latest message says, with an article attached.

Dude, I text him back, it's 8 AM. You really think I'm in the mood to read an article now?

I'm serious, he texts back immediately. It's bad. Really bad.

I scowl.

A few months back, right after Dad's death and with his scandals coming to light, our family had its fair share of bad press. But what could it be this time, months later?

I'm about to put my phone away, Landon's warning be damned, but then I catch the title of the article: The Truth about Nolan Storm.

I chuckle. This should be good. I wonder which of my disgruntled flings penned this one. Why not read it for a laugh?

Then I see the author: Sierra Hill.

No.

Fuck no.

And then I start to read:

The first thing you need to know about Nolan Storm is that he isn't what he seems. What most see is a charming man, capable, funny and ambitious; another model Storm son.

The truth is much more sinister. A serial womanizer, liar and cheater will come out in these next few paragraphs. You've been warned.

I read the rest in a daze.

It doesn't even really matter that most of the women and men she's interviewed I've either never met or are old enemies who apparently still hate me enough to lie. It doesn't even matter that everything in the article is a lie or a mischaracterization.

What matters is the author, that name I keep returning to: Sierra Hill.

I step out of the bathroom, still holding my phone, glancing from that name to her.

She's still asleep, all curled up towards where I was lying only minutes before. She has no idea.

She doesn't look like someone nursing secret hatred. She doesn't look like a liar.

But she has to be.

As I put on my jeans and shirt, it all falls into place. That article her mom mentioned her working on for that other guy. Some of the questions Sierra asked me.

Didn't she say that she had quit that job, though?

Fuck, I don't know.

She looks so sweet and unassuming asleep there, I want to shake her and yell at her and make me tell her the truth. As if, somehow, her sleeping self could be more truthful than her waking one.

Instead, I leave without a word.

I never knew Sierra Hill. That much is clear.

Back at my place, I sit in my car and call up Landon.

"You saw," he says.

"I saw," I say.

"Well, shit."

"That's one way of putting it," I say cheerily.

"You're not mad?"

"Of course I'm mad," I growl. "I just... Fuck."

"You guys are engaged," he says slowly.

"That was just a sham," I say.

"Oh." Even over the phone I can see his frown. "All of it?"

"No." I laugh. "No. You know, that's the most fucked-up thing about it, it wasn't. I..." I exhale. "Forget it. It doesn't matter now."

"You probably understand it more than I do," Landon says carefully.

"If that's your way of suggesting that I deserved this, brother, then no, I'll be frank with you, I don't understand it. I don't fucking understanding it one bit." Another exhale. "Thanks for letting me know, anyway. I've got to go."

I head up to my apartment. Once inside, I grab a chip bag someone left on a chair and start eating.

It doesn't even matter that it's some weird nouveau Lays flavor that tastes like shit. Or that my phone's ringing and it's probably her.

"You're here?" Jax says, sauntering in.

He's wearing Looney Tunes boxers I'm pretty sure Laura bought him, which means he's back to missing her again. Not that he ever really stopped.

The things we fools do for love...

"I was beginning to think you'd never be back," he jokes, helping himself to the bag of Lays. "Damn." He dumps his handful back into the bag after one bite. "Who bought these?"

"Did Laura send these as her latest punishment?" I joke.

"Hilarious," Jax says, deadpan. "Speaking of which, where's your girl? I'm expecting her to move in any day now."

Without a word, I hand him my phone with the article on it.

"Dude. As if I need to read another puff piece about how great..." He trails off as he starts to read. "Shit. Oh, shit."

When he's done, he hands me back my phone. "Fuck, man."

"I know," I just say.

"Jesus."

"I know."

I get up, head for my room.

"Want to talk about it?" he asks.

"What do you think?" I say.

I can almost feel the two factions of himself warring: the Jax that likes to stir shit up, and the one who just wants to be a good friend.

"And she didn't even deny it?" he asks.

I pause. "What are you talking about? The article has her fucking name on it, what is there for her to deny?"

He shrugs, scratching at his red hair. It looks suspiciously good—the fucker has probably been using my $35 hemp protein shampoo again. "Wouldn't hurt to hear the story behind it."

"Yeah, maybe," I say offhand.

Seeing me glaring at his hair, Jax retreats towards the bathroom. "Yeah, well, if you need me, I'm here. I'll probably be ordering burritos in a bit too."

"Thanks man," I say.

When I'm finally alone, nothing really changes.

I still don't want to call her.

Instead, I scan through my contact list, the scroll that seems never-ending. Once, Jax joked that the 'A' section of my phone was bigger than his entire contact list. As I scroll through it now, I realize he might just be right.

I've been lucky. I've been to lots of parties. Had lots of friends. Hooked up with lots of girls.

And yet, what are they now, other than names in my phone I can't place faces to?

How many nights are like that: drunken tantalizing swishes of memory, fun at the time, but, in the end, as inconsequential as a puff of smoke?

The craziest parties, the ones I heard stories about from others—about how I streaked naked down the streets of some ritzy neighborhood, or partied on a rooftop with some minor celeb—they were always amusing at the time, but—and I never told anyone this—they always left me feeling strangely empty.

Because they were never my memories. I usually didn't remember them at all. Maybe I should've cut back on the drinking. Or maybe it was the partying—when you go out more nights than not, how can you be expected to remember them all?

It wasn't like that with Sierra.

I didn't need to drink to forget. It hasn't all wisped away.

For whatever reason, it was as solid and as real as a building.

And yet, it wasn't, was it?

Somehow, it wasn't real at all. This article has proven that.

Whatever I thought we had, whatever I thought I'd endangered with this stupid fake engagement BS, was a lie.

I find my way onto my bed.

It seems I'm back to being sixteen, since the only thing I can see doing any good, making any of this better, is closing my eyes and waiting for sleep.

It's just like before. It takes forever to come, but when it does, finally, finally, it's more than worth it.

**

When I wake up, the first thing I think of is her.

I can't wait anymore. I can't make assumptions when I haven't heard the truth from her.

I have to know.

"You at home?" I ask when I call her up.

"Yeah," she says. "But why did you—"

"I'm coming over now," I say before hanging up.

I have to know.

She comes to the door, frowning, arms crossed over her chest. "I'm assuming you have some good explanation as to why you just left without a word?"

Even now, knowing what I know, it doesn't change how beautiful she is, even angry. I want to kiss every part of her, the straight lines of her eyebrows, the dapple separating her nose from her lips. I want to be stupid with her.

But first, I have to know.

"Read this." I hold out my phone.

"Nolan—" she starts.

And then she sees it and shuts up.

It takes her a few minutes to read. Then she looks at me with tears in her eyes.

"I'm so sorry," she says.

"How could you?" I say. "Was it for the money? Do you actually believe that I was capable of any of that?"

"No!" She glares at me, thrusting my phone out at me. "No, of course not. You think I actually wrote this?"

I stab my finger at the screen. "See that name there? That's yours. And believe me, I looked it up. I can't find any other Sierra Hills who are journalists."

"I started the article," she says. "But I didn't finish it. That first line is mine. The rest…" Her teeth grit together. "That asshole must have finished it himself."

"What asshole?"

She shrugs. "His name was Maurice. He had some vendetta against you, but I swear, I didn't know at first. At first, he just seemed kind of creepy but I thought it would be a harmless article—"

I have to laugh. "A harmless article, prying into my personal life—"

"I never planned to write about anything you wouldn't have wanted me to. I thought I could just focus maybe on your career, just summarizing stuff most people knew already."

"And you didn't think to tell me?" I ask flatly.

"I... I wasn't sure you'd be OK with it," she admits, looking down. "And... the money, it was really good. Insanely good, actually. I should've been more suspicious, but when my mom's house had that fire, I just thought I had to—"

"And you weren't scared of what this would mean for us, our relationship?" I say quietly.

Her gaze snaps to me, gets hard. "You're joking, right? The man who suggested us having a fake engagement is hurt because I endangered our relationship? Give me a break, Nolan."

"Jesus." I feel like throwing up my hands, but it seems overly melodramatic. "You're never going to let me live that one down, are you? Never mind that I've tried to take it back half a dozen times."

She's just shaking her head, though, keeps on shaking it. "It's too late. The fact that you were even willing to entertain the notion, it proves that this was never really real to you. Wasn't worth protecting."

"It doesn't prove a goddamn thing!" I shove my phone in her face. "This, though? Yeah. This is far worse. You, working with some guy to take me down."

She takes a step back. "So, you don't believe me, then?"

I pause. "I don't know what to believe. All I know is what I see: your name there."

She stares at me, long and hard. I finally know what shade her eyes are: it's a reflective blue, the kind that catches whatever's looking at it. A deceiving shade.

"You really think I'm capable of that?" she asks quietly.

The answer should be obvious, but she keeps the question hanging there, as if it's even a real one.

I turn to go. I heard what I needed to.

I can't even begin to think about it.

The name Maurice itches at me with a familiarity I can't place… yet.

And what Sierra's saying… I can't decide on it now.

Yeah, it seems plausible. I want to believe her.

But I need to know the truth.

Funny, I came here sure that I would find it.

"I have to go," I say, heading for the door.

"Nolan," she says, her voice a plea, a demand, an accusation. "You don't actually believe that?"

All I can say is "I don't know what I believe anymore" before I'm through the door and gone.

And still, down the elevator, out the door, in my car and even later, back in my room, her question follows me.

And I'm no closer to an answer.

CHAPTER 22

Sierra

That didn't just happen.

He didn't just...

I sit down in the hallway, my arms around my knees. I feel little again, small.

Like that time when I was four and Peyton locked me up in my parents' walk-in closet as a joke while they were outside gardening.

Like it's pitch-black everywhere and anywhere I extend my hand I'll feel something foreign, threatening. Like no matter how I cry or beg or yell, no one will hear me.

When I call them, the twins come over. They help me walk Horatio. They give me time to tell them.

When I finally do, they hug me.

"Holy moly," Josie says as we separate.

She's tried wearing her ridiculous yellow sunflower hoodie to cheer me up. Normally just the sight of it, all those smiling yellow sunflowers, makes me crack up. Not today.

"That's one way of putting it," Wynona says diplomatically.

"I can't believe that Maurice asshat would do that, though," Josie says.

"I can't believe Nolan would actually think I'd write an article like that about him," I say.

"He's an idiot," Wynona declares, getting up and heading to the kitchen, probably to find some food.

"He'll come around," Josie argues, glaring at her.

I don't say what I'm thinking: Do I even want him to?

After all we've been through, after all we've shared, that last night with the bath and stargazing and telling each other things that seemed secret, his secret admission when he thought I was asleep, I thought we were closer than this. Close enough that misunderstandings couldn't happen.

Close enough that, even if, somehow, they did, they'd fall away easily enough, as soon as we could talk to each other.

Granted, this is a singular sort of misunderstanding, but still.

Where I thought we were, there shouldn't have been doubt. Shouldn't have been uncertainty.

"Hey," Josie says, draping her arm around me. "I'm sorry."

"It's OK," I say, even though it isn't.

"You know men," she says, injecting some jokiness into her tone. "Sometimes they just need to stew it over. Realize what an idiot they've been."

I nuzzle my head onto her shoulder. "Only I'm the one who's been an idiot. With this whole Nolan thing. And taking that horrid Maurice job in the first place when it felt wrong."

"You were just trying to help your mom," Wynona says, returning with a full-on cake.

I pause, scrutinizing it. "Where did that come from?"

"I bought it," she says indifferently. "I've been having a cake craving lately anyway."

I have to chuckle. "Glad to be of service?"

"Wait till you see the caption," Josie says excitedly, ripping off the lid.

Sure enough, in rainbow swirling icing on the top, it reads: YOU GOT THIS, BITCH.

I laugh and laugh, hugging them.

"Thanks guys," I say, separating. "Should I go get..."

"Nah," Wynona says. "I think this calls for some hand slices."

"No way." I crack a grin. "But the last time we did that—"

"Yes," she says drily. "Jeremy broke up with me. Let's not revisit it."

Forming her hand into a knife, she chops a few slices. We take some.

It's yummy, but not yummy enough to totally blot today away. I'm not sure anything could.

"I just don't know if this means things are over," I say quietly, mouth full of cake.

Wynona hands me another hand-cut cake slice. I take it.

"You'll have to talk to him for that," Josie says. "But he seemed to really like you, so..."

"I don't know what I was thinking," I admit. "This relationship has been all over the place from the start."

"Relationships are hard," Josie says. "I mean, neither me nor Wyn has managed a successful one, now have we?"

Wynona takes a big swallow of cake, glaring her red-and-black-lined eyes at her sister. "Speak for yourself. Wyatt and I have been doing just fine, thank you."

Josie snorts. "You've been together for, like, five minutes."

"That's five weeks, thank you very much," Wynona says stiffly.

Josie just rolls her eyes.

"Shit, though, what are you going to do about work?" she says suddenly.

I stop chewing.

Jesus. She's right. I hadn't even thought—

"He didn't say that she was—" Wynona begins.

But I cut her off: "No, she's right. I can't go to work now. Not with things like this."

"Maybe he'll call you up to tell you that things are good?" Josie says in a hopeful tone I can tell even she doesn't believe. "Since those articles you did write him were amazing, at the end of the day."

"Maybe," I say, because I don't want to talk about it anymore.

The twins stay the night, but the next morning, they have to go to their jobs.

I walk Horatio, do some cleaning I'd been avoiding, and then it's unavoidable.

Here I am, with even less than I started with. OK, I earned some decent money and journalist experience—but at what cost?

In the afternoon, he calls me. "We should talk."

It's odd, after hearing that voice with so much emotion and good humor, hearing it lifeless like this now.

"OK," I say. "Where?"

"Your place?"

"There's a park nearby," I say. Maybe that will prevent me from having a full-blown freak out. I always have managed to stay calm better when I'm in public. "There?"

"Sure," he says. "Twenty minutes?"

"Twenty minutes," I say, and then he hangs up.

"Twenty minutes," I murmur to myself—and then race to the mirror.

It feels childish, making sure that my hair looks not-shit and my face doesn't look as kill-me-now as I'm feeling, but I do it. As if, somehow, me looking good will change his mind. As if anything will change his mind at this point.

I get to the park first. It's a laughable 'park', basically a foursquare patch of green no one cared enough to do anything else with. I sit on the only bench, and am careful not to slump.

"Hey," he says, coming to sit beside me. He doesn't look at me.

"Hey," I say.

"I'm sorry for doing the article," I say. "That's why I quit—it didn't feel right."

He nods. He's close, but not touching me. "I'm sorry for believing the worst about you. I just don't get it—why do it at all?"

"I was a little mad," I admit. It's weird, talking like this, not looking at him, gauging how he's taking it. But it's easier too. And I won't look until he will. "About the fake engagement. It seemed like you were forcing it on us just to suit your purposes. It made me question things."

"That makes sense," he says neutrally.

"But?"

"Who says there's a but?"

I chance a glance at him. Face of stone. He isn't even frowning. Just blank. Like he handed off his emotions to someone else to make better use of. "It's written all over your face."

"I don't know."

"Yes, you do." Suddenly, maybe it's the growing dark, or how he's not taking my hand, I feel bold. Fuck it. "Tell me. You knew about this whole will thing the whole time. Can you tell me for sure that it didn't influence you pursuing me and things getting more serious between us?"

The birds chatter, and I see a flit of one—a chickadee. They giggle over our dour expressions. But Nolan remains silent, and I can't accept how loudly that silence says: No.

"Nolan."

"I don't trust you," he says suddenly.

"And I don't trust you," I say, realizing it as I say it. "Now tell me, can you say for certain that your dad's will didn't influence you pursuing me, us getting serious?"

It comes out a bit louder than an exhale, quieter than normal speech: "No."

I wait, for him to explain it or joke it away, like he normally does. For him to make it better. But he just sits there, as if he knows what I'm going to say, wants me to say it, even.

"So, then that's it," I say quietly. "This is it?"

I can hear the shrug of his powerful shoulders on the bench beside me. "If you say so."

"If I say so." Next second, I'm on my feet, mad, raging, smack-him, yell-level mad. "You're the one who said you can't trust me!"

"You said it too."

"You said it first, and, I have good reason."

He rises too, finally looks me in the eye. It's worse. There's nothing there: no pain, no anger, no sadness. I don't know what happened to Nolan Storm, but he's not in this man before me. This shell.

"And I don't?" he says.

"I didn't say that," I say.

I pause again.

It occurs to me then that I'm caught in the same stupidity. Waiting for Nolan to make it better, make it right. When he was the one to make it wrong in the first place.

"So then," I say. "We should end it."

When he doesn't answer again, this time I don't wait. I leave.

I'm done waiting for Nolan Storm to make the right choice. To fight for us.

And yet, even as I finally do the right thing—way too late, of course—I still mess it up. Halfway back to my place, and then again at my building's door, I pause, look back.

And still, even though I knew what I would find, knew it was pointless, still I'm surprised when I don't see him there.

That he didn't follow.

That he's really not going to make any of this better.

CHAPTER 23

Nolan

"Helloooo? Nolan?" Jax waves a freckled hand in front of my face.

I rise, scowling. "Need to take a piss."

I stalk off.

It's not the first time I've zoned out during this dinner. It probably won't be the last, either.

Why the fuck did I think going on a double date would be a good idea now?

Maybe because Jax goaded me into it, reminding me that it's been a month since Sierra and I stopped seeing each other.

One month... Jesus, has it really been that long?

Instead of heading to the bathroom, though, I head outside.

The fresh air isn't so fresh—it stinks of car exhaust and the Cinnabon across the street. A weird combo. I almost feel hungry for car exhaust.

My head's all messed up these days.

Still, I go through the motions and pretend I'm not. I land on her name—Sierra Hill—as if I'll finally delete her out of my phone, call her up, who knows.

I don't do either, of course.

Still back on that bench, Nolan, boy...

Not wanting to leave, not wanting to stay.

That's the thing about uncertainty: it's always rife with possibility, potential. Make a choice and you're locked and loaded, consequences included.

Sierra was right to leave, to say what she did. Even if I didn't want her to, she was right, maybe.

How could we go back to how it was, when we didn't trust each other?

And what had I expected, anyway?

Relationships don't work. For every happy old couple you see, there are five or more who've separated and are living out the rest of their days as lonely, scarred husks, or are still together but hate each other's guts.

Relationships aren't worth the risk.

Even now, after only a few months with her, look what I am. A pathetic sack of shit, unable to bang another girl, unable to even delete Sierra out of my phone.

Sierra Hill…

I stalk back into the restaurant.

No point in hanging out outside mulling over what I already know.

That I need to fucking let go, and I can't.

"There he is," Jax says, pushing a freshly-ordered cocktail in front of me. "We got you something."

"Something to cheer you up," the pretty Asian girl beside me says, squeezing my hand. "Jax told us what you're going through."

"It's nothing," I say.

"You poor thing." Under the table, she pats my leg.

I sip at my drink, and I can almost see it now. How tonight will end—how ten dozen other tonights have ended, at least before Sierra: We'll drink until we're buzzed, then head over to a club. Jax will order us all shots, or maybe it'll be me. He'll dance with his girl, I'll dance with mine. Maybe we'll see some familiar faces in the crowd, maybe not.

The after party will be at ours, filled with more people we don't know than we do. Someone will order pizza, someone else will propose shots. And then me and this girl in my bed, this girl I've been with countless times before.

"It's not nothing," Jax argues. "There's that article BS. Then your foreman quitting. You're going through a lot."

I put my drink down, surprised that I finished it in virtually one swig. "Thanks for the reminder."

He shrugs. "It's why I bought you this pity drink."

"You planning on taking me out tonight too?" I flutter my lashes at him.

If tonight's going to go like all the other tonights, I might as well go along with it. Maybe it will help, make things more like before.

"Darling," Jax quips, raising his glass to me. "Of course. The two wretches that we are."

The girls laugh dutifully. We've all done this before, gone through the motions.

My phone goes off.

I grab it faster than normal. Even now, some idiot part of my brain expects to see her name on the screen.

It's only Greyson, though.

"Got a minute?" he says. "I've got news."

"Sure," I say, making an apologetic face to the others as I head back outside.

I could probably stay in the restaurant and take the call. It's not like it's super loud in here or anything. Just that at him saying 'I've got news', I want to have enough air to think it over, whatever this news is.

It can't be about Emerson—he's been golden since that overdose mishap. It can't be about Dad's will, either—that's old news by now.

"Got any plans next week?" he asks.

I have to laugh mirthlessly. "You didn't hear that my foreman quit? Right when the renos were finally starting to get somewhere. I'm going to be stuck at the club sorting out the mess practically 24/7 for the next few weeks."

"Ah," he says. "You sure you can't get away?"

"What's this about?" I ask.

"Just—Storm TV got renewed for a third season. We're heading to Tahiti. I'm taking the whole family. Landon, Emerson and the others are coming too."

"Shit," I say.

"You could come," he says.

"No," I say, scowling. "I can't. I want to, I just can't afford the renos being any more behind than they already are."

"Shit," Greyson says. "I'd put it off, I just booked the flights and everything already."

"It's OK," I say. "Maybe if I can get the construction crew working at a good pace, I could jet down for the last day or something like that. Though I doubt it."

"You do what you have to," Greyson says. "Business first, I get it. You've got a lot on your plate right now."

"Thanks," I say.

"Have you been in touch with her?" he asks.

"Who?" I ask, although my scowl already knows.

"You know who."

The sidewalk I'm standing on is all rough and cracked. I've wandered only a block away from the restaurant, and yet it seems like I'm in another country, one where the pigeons striding down the center of the sidewalk own this place, and the dirty hobos gathered off to the side are their henchmen.

"No," I finally say.

"You sure that's for the best?" His tone is light, almost casual, but it still makes my fists clench.

"No, I'm not," I say coolly. "You have something to say about it?"

"I don't pretend to be some expert on love," Greyson says. "Just— when you brought her over—"

"A mistake," I cut him off.

"Maybe," he says, though he doesn't sound like he believes it. "You just seemed... happy."

"And I don't normally?"

"Not always."

"Well."

In the background, I can hear Harley humming along to some Beatles song.

It swipes at me with no warning: I wonder what Sierra's doing right now?

Writing one of her articles? Dining with the twins? On a date with some guy who makes her laugh more than I did?

"Anyway," he says, "I think you should talk to her. See if you can work things out. But you know me."

"A regular old romantic," I quip.

"Not before Harley," he says, and he has a point. I remember the years when Greyson didn't even have a serious girlfriend, let alone a wife. "There's just some women you meet, who change you. You can't let them go. You…"

"Aren't you sweet," Harley coos from the background. "I'm definitely making those cookies you like tonight! Naked."

"Babe," Greyson says. "Nolan can hear—"

"I support all naked cookie making," I announce loudly with a laugh.

"Don't imagine my wife naked," Greyson growls.

"She was the one who said it," I say innocently.

"Yeah, yeah."

"I appreciate the advice, big broski, really," I tell him. "But trust me, if you'd been there, you'd know. It's over between Sierra and I."

"Alright, if you say so." Greyson's tone is the verbal equivalent of shrugged shoulders.

"Thanks for including me in the vacation plans, though I'll have to pass," I say. "Fucking renos."

"Good luck," he says. "See ya."

"See ya," I say, hanging up.

I head back to the restaurant before I can mull over what he said about Sierra and I.

Not that it'll take much mulling.

Sierra and I are over. End of story.

Back inside, I stop at the head of our table. "Now, who's up for shots at Benji's?"

What I need for tonight is another blur to add to a swish of them. Get back on my game.

Another hookup. Another night to put between me and her.

The rest of the night goes more or less as planned. We hit up another club and then another.

The girls get drunker, we get drunker.

Except, when my girl starts dancing on me, I have to go get another drink. It happens the next time too.

Finally, I stalk outside. I go linger around some 20-something smokers, strike up a conversation for no reason.

So that I don't have to think about it, the question that keeps returning to me as persistent as an itch: What the fuck is wrong with me?

CHAPTER 24

Sierra

Kill. Me. Now.

"Hi, how can I help you?" I say instead to an approaching blonde couple that look like they want to be here as little as I do.

"Sierra, Sierra, Sierra," Raymond says, escorting me off to the side with a very unnecessary hairy hand on my shoulder, while Jina takes over from me to take their orders. "What did we say about enthusiasm? We want people to want to order here. Not to scare them away."

Since I'm in no mood to smile, I focus my energies on at least not outright glaring at him.

Even though I despise everything about him, from his wispy mustache to his watery eyes to his mayonnaise breath.

To think I forgot how much I hated working here. Hated Raymond himself. I've been here all of two hours, and he's already managed to be creepy half a dozen times.

But the bills won't pay themselves, I remind myself firmly.

After giving all the money I made on the Nolan job to my mom to help pay for fixing her house, I'm pretty much back to square one. A few weeks of desperately shooting out my resume, with no response, has left me here.

Maybe one day I can break into the journalism field. Just not today.

"Oh, look who it is?" a horribly familiar voice says.

Oh no. Oh please God no.

"You know her?" Raymond says, smiling at me like he's doing me a favor. "You can help her if you like."

"No, I'd really rather not," I say. "Actually, come to think of it, I have to go to the bathroom and—"

"We're not paying you to go to the bathroom," Raymond says with a firm shove that sends me staggering to the counter.

And then, here I am, behind the counter and facing down Peyton. My sister. AKA the last person I want to be seeing right now.

"What a surprise," Peyton coos, clearly delighted. "When Mom mentioned it, I knew I just had to stop by."

She leans in with a thrilled concern on her perfectly made-up face. "Of course, it's not quite as nice as those journalism jobs you had, but then again, don't we all need a little bit of humbling now and then?"

"What do you want, Peyton?" I say in a flat monotone.

I'm not sure of Pancake House's exact employee guidelines, but I'm pretty sure chucking a pancake into your bitchy sister's face isn't allowed.

"Oh, not to order anything here." Tight smile. "Wouldn't want to waste my calories. Oh, and I heard about your breakup—so sad. I mean, ensnaring a guy that good and then just losing him..."

That's it.

I lean forward to hiss, "Eat shit."

Peyton steps back, hand flying to her mouth. "What did you say?"

I bear my teeth into a smile as my hand jerks up in a wave. "Have a nice day!"

She pauses, clearly unsure whether it would be worse for me to lose my shit job or be stuck here. Finally, apparently deciding the latter, she storms out.

"Huh," Raymond says, fleshy mouth lolling. "That your sister, eh?"

"Yep," I say. "That's her."

After another few minutes of useless chitchat and unnecessary shoulder maneuvering, Raymond finds something to do in the back and leaves me alone. Just in time, too—the twins show up.

"Thank God," I say, coming to the counter.

Josie makes a sympathetic face. "That bad, eh? I told you, if you just wait a few weeks, I could probably get you in at the nursery when Sheila goes on maternity leave."

"I don't have a few weeks," I remind her. "Rent is due next week, and last time Yurk sent me a nice little letter saying one more late payment and he's throwing my stuff on the curb."

"Fucking Yurk," Wynona mutters with a shake of her head.

"Is it really that bad?" Josie says, clearly trying to ease her conscience.

"Well, let's see," I say. "So far, Raymond has been a creep, Peyton has visited and rubbed this job and me and Nolan breaking up in my face, and I had one customer berate me and call me a 'menace to society' because our in-store price is different from our online one. So, let's just say that I've had better days."

"Well," Josie says, trying to smile. "At least you only have... two more hours left?"

"Small blessings," I agree, nodding fervently.

"About Nolan," Wynona says through her frown. "Still no word from him?"

"Nope," I say. "Not that I expected any. If you guys had been there at the park, you would've gotten it. It was like he wasn't even the same person at all."

"Jesus," Josie says. "And you didn't even write that article."

"I know," I say. "I think he had trust issues anyway, and that thing didn't help. I just..."

I trail off.

Sure, the twins are my best friends, but the middle of the work day when I might have to face Raymond or customers at any point probably isn't the best time to admit that I expected so much more from Nolan.

That I thought we had something. Something that couldn't be broken easily. That a stupid part of me is still waiting for him to call.

Yeah, I was the one to suggest us ending things, but I didn't expect him to just accept it. To just walk away from us as if it never meant anything.

"I'll have an extra-large pancake with peanut butter, please," Josie says suddenly, face dropping.

Shit. Raymond.

"Of course," I say, with a smile. "Coming right up."

Once the twins take their pancakes and leave (since Raymond is lingering like a fat fruit fly), the next few hours crawl along like a turtle stuck in molasses. By the time my shift is over, I stumble home in a daze, and am about to collapse onto my couch when I step in—

"Horatio! No!" I yell.

But it's too late. I've stepped in liquidy shit and—

"You dick!" I yell.

He apparently had a diarrhea attack all over my floor because he ate…

A glance at the kitchen and I chuck my purse at the wall. "For fuck's sake!"

The bastard somehow got into my last bag of ramen. The one that's supposed to last me until next week.

Shit-smeared foot be damned, I collapse onto the couch.

At this point, I wouldn't be surprised if the ceiling fell in.

CHAPTER 25

Nolan

Today's the day.

Three months after my dad's will. Tomorrow, I'll lose my inheritance.

Tomorrow, I might just call her, though.

I've been playing with the idea for the past few weeks. Had her number dialed half a dozen times.

She's left me no choice. She hasn't called. She hasn't texted.

And it's not like I can get on with my life without her. I've tried. I've tried going out, partying. It's not the same. Nothing is.

Today, though, I'm just going to go to our restaurant and have a burger. Maybe even a beer.

Think about how I'll win her back—if I even should. Being with her fucks with my head, after all.

Figuring out how I'm going to fund the rest of the renovations would be nice too. I've finally got the boys on a good pace, but them not getting paid would 10/10 screw it up. I can't afford to have the club closed much longer, and I'd rather not have to borrow money from any of my brothers, even if this is a family establishment.

One step through the club's front doors, and I freeze.

No fucking way.

But—mahogany swish of hair—Coke bottle body my hands itch to wrap around—it is.

It's her.

I freeze.

What are the fucking odds?

I almost turn around.

Not today—I'm not ready—

But before I can decide, I blurt out: "Sierra?"

She turns around, gapes at me for half a minute.

When she finally finds her voice, she says, "Oh. Sorry, I—I'm just here to pick up my cardigan."

"Oh," I say.

Were her eyes always that blue and big? Was she always so gorgeous and poised?

Fuck me.

She starts to turn away.

"I was going to call," I blurt out. "I almost did."

She pauses.

"Why didn't you?" she asks.

"Why did you suggest ending things?" I shoot back.

Even from her profile, I can see her expression go pained. "You thought I was capable of... then the fake engagement..." She whips her head to face me, with a look that's sad and wistful. "How can we have something if neither of us trusts the other?"

It makes sense, except—

"How can we know that we can't make it work if we don't try?" I ask.

The sadness in her eyes wavers as she says, "What are you saying?"

"I'm saying let's try." I try to smile, but something tells me I won't be able to until I have her answer.

Her eyes widen slightly, then narrow. "What day is it?"

"What are you talking about?"

She strides past me, already shaking her head. "You know what, I'm not sure I can do this. Not with your dad's will thing still up in the air."

"The last day is today," I answer her. "For the will thing."

She freezes, her upper lip curling. "So, you're saying, let's do the fake engagement and—"

"No." Now it's my turn to snap. "If you gave me a second to explain…"

She swallows, nodding a little. "I… just need to think. OK? This is all so sudden."

"Sure," I say, even though part of me feels dull and swollen and slack, like I've lost her again. "Right."

I let her walk out the door, and I don't follow her.

I can't stop myself from getting out my phone and texting her, though: Am I allowed to text you?

I'm putting my phone back in my pocket, hardly expecting a response, when: If I said no would you really stop?

I grin. No. Then: How long do you need to think?

—Would a few hours be too much to ask?

Depends, I text back. Does texting stop you from thinking?

—You really are incorrigible, you know that?

I've been called worse.

And suddenly, I can't stand here anymore. Maybe it isn't fair to her. Probably I'm being selfish. But I need to see her one last time.

I rush outside and hurry after her down the sidewalk.

She turns around, her "Nolan!" both scolding and pleased, surprised and frustrated.

My lips sweep to hers.

For a few perfect seconds, everything is how it was before.

Her lips feel so good against mine, move so well with mine.

But then she pulls away, eyes guarded. "Nolan, what—"

Next thing I know, I'm on one knee. "Sierra, will you make me the happiest man in the world, and go with me to Spain tomorrow?"

Her mouth can't decide whether to be enraged or overjoyed. "For a wedding?"

I chuckle. "Whoa there. Wine and dine me first. No. Greyson recently bought a nice old house there and invited me to check it out."

She stands there, as if still waiting for the punchline.

"In other words," I say. "I'd like to treat you to a nice vacation—if you'll accept."

"But what about your father's will and all the money?" she asks.

I rise with a shrug. "Fuck it. I've made my way before, and I can again. It won't be easy, but I'll manage."

Her forehead furrows. "So, that's it, then?"

"What?" I cock my head at her. "You only want to be with me if I'm stinking rich?"

"No!" she declares angrily.

"Then say yes," I say easily.

"Yes," she says, with a little laugh. "Yes, let's do it, let's go."

"Right answer," I murmur, as I lean in to cover her lips with mine.

For the first time in a long time, I know. Everything is going to be fucking fine.

EPILOGUE

Sierra

Six Months Later...

Nolan nudges me. "What you thinking?"

"Just"—I have to laugh—"I can't believe this is my life."

Straightening, Nolan nods. "You are lucky to be with me."

I snort, nudging him back. "Conceited much?"

He gives me a kiss on the cheek. "OK, OK, I'm the lucky one."

"That's better," I say, and we both laugh. "Although I can't believe they finished this center so quickly."

"Connections," Nolan says with a pleased shrug of his powerful shoulders. "Maybe Dad didn't leave me any money, but he left me those at least. Plus, even the military agreed there is a huge need for something like this. Us ex-military people have been getting the shaft for generations."

I squeeze his arm. "Not anymore, though. Or at least not as much."

Nolan nods with a smile. "That's the idea. Education and care is the way to go. I'm just glad I can help."

And what help it is: the Storm Center for Military Personnel has already employed hundreds of the best minds in psychology and physiotherapy to help rehabilitate current and former service members. Nolan's been stopping in here several times a week, and it shows. The building itself is gorgeous, all airy with walls and ceiling of stunning glass, while the project hurried to completion without so much as a hitch. Nolan jokes that they used Amish, and that's why it went so fast. But considering the timeline, I'm not sure how much of a joke that really was.

As we near the entrance and the tour winds up, Nolan checks his phone. "Shit—we better go, or we'll be late."

"You couldn't have booked the comedy club's reopening party on a different date from the tour?" I tease him.

"Now, that would be no fun," he protests, with a shake of his long, dark-haired head.

He gives our regards and goodbyes to the organizers, then we hurry off to the Storm Comedy Club.

"I can't believe the renovations are finally done," Nolan admits as he drives us there in his Porsche. "I was starting to think you and I would have seven children and a couple of grandchildren before it finally got finished."

I chuckle, carefully giving him a side-eye. "I thought you said that you weren't 100% about wanting kids at all."

"It was just an expression," Nolan says, then shrugs. "Although, come to think of it, maybe in another year or so wouldn't be a bad time."

"Oh yeah?" I say, trying to keep the excitement out of my voice, but grinning all the same.

"Yeah," he says, grinning too.

"Good," I say.

"Good," he says.

We both laugh.

"I'm just excited to see your first article for the Times," Nolan comments as we near the club. "You going to do a follow-up to your Nolan masterpiece?"

I shoot him a cutting glare. "I thought we agreed not to mention that."

He chuckles a little. "I almost forgot to tell you—I figured out why that name Maurice rang a bell. I talked to Jax and it turns out I unknowingly stole his fiancee a few years ago. The guy has hated my guts ever since. And no, I didn't know she had a fiance when I hooked up with her."

"Aren't you just a catch," I comment.

He just grins. "Tell me about it."

A few minutes later, we're walking into the Comedy Club, which is packed. Paparazzi, caterers, a DJ, some comedians and celebrities, and, of course, our friends and family.

All the Storm brothers and their spouses are delighted to see me, while Mom had the foresight not to bring Peyton. After Peyton tried seducing Nolan one night while claiming to be planning my surprise birthday party, let's just say that Mom finally agrees that she's a vile bitch.

Nolan is almost immediately whisked away by some friends, not that I mind. The twins have already saved me some cupcakes.

Josie is holding hers like she's afraid to eat it. "I'm pretty sure this costs as much as my sink."

She has a point. The thing is a work of art—flecked with gold, while the wrapper looks to be made of gold lace.

Wynona grabs it and pops it in her mouth. "Probably."

"You bitch!" Josie grumbles, then turns to me. "Have you told him yet?"

"Shh!" I scold her. "You promised. No mentioning it in public."

"Please." Josie rolls her eyes. "The only one in earshot is my future husband."

"Huh?" I say, eyeing the only person standing near us: a pale man who looks like a modern vampire.

He finally wanders off, looking disappointed for some reason.

Wynona chuckles. "He and Josie have been eye-fucking all night. It's only a matter of time."

"Better than how you've been giving Emerson a death glare for the past hour," Josie says smoothly.

An oddly pained expression comes over Wynona's face.

"Guys?" I say.

"She's just having a bad day," Josie says, a little too readily, it seems to me.

Or maybe my judgment is off from all the late nights I've had recently, unable to sleep.

How could I with the big news I have for Nolan?

"First though," Josie says firmly, as though sniffing out my thoughts, "you have to tell us: Did you tell him?"

"Oh, you mean in between our tour of his new center and zooming over here?" I say. "No, shockingly, I didn't."

"Told you," Wynona singsongs as she helps herself to another cupcake. "She's scared."

"I am not." I glare at both of them. "I'm just waiting for the right time."

"You've known for a week," Josie points out. "At this rate, the right time will be when you're in the delivery room."

"No," I say. "I just didn't want to tell him when he's all caught up with last-minute preparations for the center opening and the comedy club reopening party."

"You're scared," the twins singsong evilly.

"If I was before," I grumble, crossing my arms over my chest, "then I'm definitely not now. Nolan basically said that kids in the next year wouldn't be horrible."

"And that wasn't the right time to tell him?" Josie presses.

"No," I say, glancing over to find the pale man, waiting awkwardly by a chocolate fruit fountain. I shoo away Josie. "Now go. God knows we need you to have a man so we can plan our three couples vacation."

Josie snorts, although she does head off towards Mr. Vamp. "Glad that my welfare is so important to you two."

"We love you," Wynona says, deadpan.

"How's Horatio doing?" I ask her. "I still feel bad about giving him up."

"You kidding me?" Wynona says. "The little guy is a new dog. He's fallen in love with Winston, and he hasn't shit inside since he arrived here. You did the right thing."

"Wow," I say. "Really? I guess so, then."

The rest of the party Nolan spends with me. We get some pictures taken and try some of the delicious food before Nolan finally pulls me away.

"I thought I'd never get a chance, at this rate," he says, grinning. "I have another surprise for you."

I grin. "Oh?"

"Have any plans tonight?" he asks casually.

"Maybe," I say, just as casually.

"Well, drop them, because I have something to show you."

He pulls me outside to see, on the top of the Storm comedy club, a freaking helicopter.

"No way," I say, half laughing.

"You're right. My bad—that must be Jax's helicopter."

I yank his arm. "Nolan, explain!"

He chuckles. "I never mentioned that tropical island I bought you for your birthday?"

"My birthday is next week, but no."

"The one that already has a villa on it, that we're going to tonight?"

"This is not funny," I growl.

"But I'm not joking!" he insists.

"What?!?" I exclaim. "But my stuff…"

Nolan gestures to the helicopter. "Already packed and loaded. Now, you have any other excuses?"

I have to smile. "No?"

"Good." He takes my hand. "Then let's go."

And we do. The helicopter is pure luxury: gold-colored leather and overflowing baskets of fruit inside.

Arriving at the villa is nothing less than a fairy tale. The 60,000-square foot property boasts a gorgeous garden of hedges shaped like dolphins and roses of every color of the rainbow, fountains and high-ceilinged rooms that seem like they belong more in some lifestyle magazine than real life.

By the time we finally collapse into bed, there's no doubt in my mind: it's time.

"I have something to tell you," I say.

"You like it?" Nolan says, rolling over to face me.

"Does that really need to be said?" I say, with a little laugh.

"First, though, can I show you something?" he asks, taking my hand.

By now, it's night outside, although not so dark that I can't see the path of rose petals Nolan's leading me down.

"Nolan, what?" I ask.

"You'll see," is all he says.

And I do. There in the center of the gardens, by candlelight, Nolan gets down on one knee. "When I met you, Sierra, I didn't know what love is. I didn't think that relationships were worth it. I didn't think my girl was out there. But then I met you. I... I'm usually good with words, but I don't know how to make you get it. That I want to spend the rest of my life with you. That there's nothing funny about it. I love you, Sierra. Will you be my wife?"

This time, I don't need to even pause to think. I take his hand and squeeze it. "Yes, of course yes! But..."

I get down on one knee. Nolan goggles at me. "This isn't how the proposal is supposed to go."

"You'll see," is all I say.

"Nolan," I ask, cutting to the chase. "Will you be the father of our child?"

A smile jumps onto his face. "You want to get pregnant?"

A smile jumps onto mine. "Guess again."

"You are pregnant," he corrects, and I nod.

He laughs, an overjoyed full-bellied sound, leaning over to hug me. "Thank God for you."

"Thank God for you," I say, right before our lips meet.

~The End~

If you LOVED Just Pretend, be sure to check out His Second Chance!

It's a fun and flirty hot romance read filled with page melting heat, lots of teasing, drama and some sugar sweet moments guaranteed to leave you with a very satisfying happily-ever-after.

Click Here and Get His Second Chance Now!

HIS SECOND CHANCE SNEAK PEEK

I just saw my first love turned enemy at my best friend's wedding.
When he lands back in my bed, I'm left thinking,
This could be our second chance at love.
Or a level 10 disaster waiting to happen...

After 5 long years, our eyes locked once again.

He knows what he's doing.

Same silky smooth voice.

Same way of going after *exactly* what he wants.

Control is gone.

In its place is just one thing.

Desire.

Red and hot.

He wants me.

I want him.

My guard is up.

I might trust my body to him.

But my heart?

He'll have to work much harder for that.

Especially now that he's given me something special to carry.

What will he do when I tell him?

Get His Second Chance Now

https://www.ashleepriceromanceauthor.com/product/his-second-chance-an-enemies-to-lovers-romance-love-comes-to-town-book-4/

Chapter 1

Wynona

He wouldn't dare.

But the longer I sit on my cushioned wicker seat, the harder it is to deny it.

I grip the monogrammed S&N cupcake I'm holding hard.

Whoever's wearing five times more skunk-esque perfume than need be, I want to punch. Almost as much as I want to punch him.

That's our song, alright.

He doesn't say the words, but he doesn't need to. As his hands glide over the piano keys, I can hear them in my head:

Past, present, future, you are

Whenever I'm far

...away

It's time to say

I gotta get back to you

I gotta get back to you...

"Liar," I hiss under my breath.

And the way he's looking at me, that beautiful sculpted face, with its tousled blond hair and blue eyes I already know all too well can be about fifteen different shades depending on his mood...

Emerson Fucking Storm.

The whole reason I shouldn't have come.

But then again, Sierra Hill- no, now Sierra Storm is my best friend. I couldn't abandon her at her wedding, of all times.

Now, get this, the song's over and done with and Emerson is the one walking off, looking thoughtful and sad.

As if he was the one who'd had the past cruelly dredged up.

He tries looking my way, but I'm prepared. I've had 26 years to perfect this glare of mine.

If glares could kill, mine would've made Emerson explode in a nice puff of red and black confetti so a nice old janitor who looks like Bill Nye could sweep him up.

Alas, no such luck.

"Uh, Winnie?" Josie whispers, elbowing me.

"What?" I snap.

Her sparkly pale face, with its powdery blue sparkly eye shadow and, you guessed it, sparkly pink gloss, has a holier-than-thou expression I'm so not in the mood for. "If you really hate the cupcakes you could, you know, just not take one?"

I glare at her, until I realize that she has a point.

That makes two cupcakes I've smooshed to an untimely death on my gold-rimmed plate.

...Whoops.

"Maybe we should get drunker?" Josie suggests with a quirked strawberry-blonde eyebrow, her eyes already on the bar.

I quirk my own black-lined eyebrow back at her. "Were you not there when Sierra gave her very kind, very firm talk about when to get shit-faced and when not to?"

"The wedding's over with," she points out. "They're about to start the music, now that Emerson has played a few pieces. I'd say now is as good a time as any."

I make a skeptical noise.

"Suit yourself," Josie says, bobbing upright with more energy than I've had since I was about four years old. "I, for one, am going to enjoy tonight."

I wave at her. "Have funnnnn."

Josie pauses, guilt finding its way onto her cheerful face as she leans in. "I'm sorry, Wyn. I know this is hard. Maybe if you just—"

"No," I say sharply, shaking my head for emphasis. "We already discussed this."

Josie says loudly. "I know. But if you just told Sierra—"

"Told me what?" Sierra says, her gorgeous shimmering poof of a wedding gown billowing around her as she approaches our table.

"Nothing," Josie and I trill at the same time.

Sierra just laughs, although her gaze softens when it stops on me. "Honestly, Wyn, if you have to go off and cry, or need me to be there for you, I can be. Even if it's my wedding day, you just went through the breakup of all breakups."

Halfway through her speech, I'm already shaking my head. "No can do, Sierra. I am a selfish bitch—but not that much of a selfish bitch."

"Honestly," she says, smile broadening as she sneaks a look back at her new husband, Nolan. "Nothing could ruin today for me. And after you made that... sacrifice as far as the bridesmaid's dress is concerned..."

I aim a glare at Josie, the one who chose it, who's smiling innocently. "Don't worry, I don't blame you for the..." *monstrosity, mockery, punishment* "...color."

Just then, the first song of the night booms on: *Oh, listen up, here's a story, about a little guy that lives in a blue world...*

Sierra throws her perfectly done red-brown hair back and cackles as she looks at me. "That song: 'Blue'? You didn't!"

"I did," I say, smiling despite myself as I rise. "I had to get some good stuff on that playlist, with all the Michael Bublé, Backstreet Boys and Spice Girls Josie insisted on slipping in there."

"I've heard you singing 'Stop Right Now' in the shower," Josie accuses me blandly, rising too.

I just shrug, although she has a point. "There's no telling what drunk me will do."

And that's the problem, isn't it?

The reason I can't drink away my sorrows, as per usual.

Because there is a big mistake here I have no plans to repeat.

And his name is Emerson Storm.

But, as Sierra, Josie and I get to the dance floor and groove our hearts out, and I grab one more drink—just one—I almost forget.

I'm almost back there. Sixteen years old at the first rave I snuck into with them. We all had matching pink synthetic wigs and white velvet American Apparel dresses, and we spent most of the night exploring the abandoned factory the rave was in, when we weren't giggling at any guy who tried to talk to us or dancing so hard we were out of breath after. We requested this song from the DJ so many times he ended up flipping us off.

We were still immature, stupid kids then. Things were still easy in the way they are before you grow up.

When the song's done, I'm already dead tired. Might be thanks to the part when we all started jumping franticly. Or where Josie and I lifted Sierra to our shoulders, the three of us laughing and laughing.

Or maybe it's how, near the end of the song, I saw him.

Off to the side, looking at me as if I was some kind of physical barrier between him and the dance floor. As if I was the one who ruined things all those years ago.

"I'm going to take a breather," I tell my friends, even though we're already outside, and it's already cool.

But a breather for me means—has always meant—being alone. Quiet. Having space to think.

Even though that last part rarely does me much good.

It takes me a few minutes of walking down the beach, away from the music and the happy wedding party, away from the odd hotel beach lounger and romantic couple, before I really am alone. Finally.

I plonk my butt in the sand and stare out into the roving waves. Advance, advance, advance... crash.

Closer, closer, closer... crash.

A lone gull from somewhere wheels. Somewhere further off, someone whoops.

I don't know why, but I've never felt lonelier then when I hear other people having fun and I'm not.

I close my eyes and inhale deeply.

I can smell the salt in the air, taste it.

I let my heeled feet dig into the sand, let my head fall back.

Ah, now this—this was exactly what I needed.

Suddenly, my back stiffens.

My eyes are closed, and there hasn't been so much as a sound or murmur out of place, yet... I know.

Someone's here.

"Imagine seeing you here," an all-too-familiar voice says.

Get His Second Chance Now

https://www.ashleepriceromanceauthor.com/product/his-second-chance-an-enemies-to-lovers-romance-love-comes-to-town-book-4/

GET MORE FROM ASHLEE PRICE

Amazon lists millions of titles, and I'm happy you discovered this one.

But if you'd like to know when I release a new book, instead of leaving it up to chance, sign up for my newsletter.

I'll send you an email when my latest release goes live.

https://www.ashleepriceromanceauthor.com/signup/